Dark Horse

Jean Slaughter Doty

Dark
Horse

Illustrated by Dorothy Haskell Chhuy

William Morrow and Company
New York 1983

Printed in the United States of America.

10 9 8 7 6 5 4 3

Library of Congress Cataloging in Publication Data
Doty, Jean Slaughter, 1924–   Dark horse.
Summary: A special brown horse helps Abby realize her dream of taking part
in first-class competition riding. 1. Horses—Juvenile fiction. [1. Horses—Fic-
tion. 2. Horsemanship—Fiction] I. Chhuy, Dorothy Haskell, ill. II. Title.
PZ10.3.D7197Dar   1983   [Fic]   82-21651
ISBN 0-688-01703-7

To Pat—who was there.
To another Sandy, who owed me one.
—and to the good field hunters, for their love
of the sport,
who are not the glory horses.

1

I heard the horse van shifting gears as it rumbled over the bridge at the bottom of the hill. The sound of the engine changed to a whine as the van turned through the farm gates.

The stables were quiet. I had fed all the horses and they had finished their evening grain. Now they were rustling their hay contentedly and the only sounds were the whispers of hay and the skitter of the barn cat's kittens playing in the stable aisle.

I squeezed the suds out of the sponge and tossed it into the tack room sink. The saddle I was cleaning could wait. I rubbed my hands dry on my jeans and hurried to the stable door.

The battered gray van was grinding up the last of the hill. It drew to a shuddering stop in the stable driveway. My heart gave its familiar leap of anticipation. A new vanload of horses and ponies was always exciting, no matter how many I'd seen come in during the few months since we'd moved to our new house and I'd started helping here at High Hickory Farms.

The van was silent except for the ticking of its cooling engine. The horses in it must be tired. I knew they'd come a long way. The driver opened the door of the cab and swung to the ground, moving his shoulders stiffly.

"Hi there, Abby," he said. "Is the big boss around?"

"Hi, Carl." I stood on tiptoe as though this could possibly help me see through the van's high, streaky windows. "Russ isn't here. He had to go with the trailer to pick up a client's horse. It's Donna's day off, and the other grooms have already gone home. I told Russ I'd stay on in case you got here before he came back. What have you got for us this trip?"

"I've got the gray Connemara pony Russ wanted me to pick up in Vermont for him, and a couple of others I thought he might want to see. And a broodmare I'm supposed to take on down to Pennsylvania tomorrow."

I helped Carl open the side doors and pull the heavy van ramp to the ground. We put the side wings of the ramp in place and I followed Carl eagerly up the rough matting, into the dim shadows of the van.

"Here, Abby, you take the Connemara out. He won't give you any trouble."

I made a face behind his back but didn't say anything. Carl, like a lot of older horsemen, couldn't accept a girl just in junior high school handling anything more than an ancient small pony; but I had been helping in stables, mucking stalls and grooming and riding horses and ponies, ever since I was big enough to hold a pitchfork.

I clipped a lead rope to the halter of the big gray pony and led him out of the narrow van stall and down the ramp. The pony looked nice enough, as far as I could tell, though his winter coat made him look more like a polar bear. He was huge, as big as a pony could be with-

2

out being a horse, I guessed. I put him into one of the stalls that had been freshly bedded, waiting for the new arrivals.

Carl was bringing a bay Thoroughbred mare down the ramp as I hurried back to the van. She was wide and round, heavy in foal, and Carl steadied her anxiously.

"The owners of this mare are crazy to ship her this far," he said as he led the mare safely down to the level surface of the driveway. "She's due to have her foal any day now."

I held the weary mare's lead rope while Carl checked her over. "Owners," Carl said in disgust. "It wouldn't hurt for some of them to learn more about horses. They ship them around like boxes of cheese."

He patted the mare softly. "Gently does it, old girl," he said. "We may make it through to Pennsylvania, after all." He gave me a doubtful look. "Can you put her away all right?"

"I think I can handle it," I said, trying not to smile. I coaxed the tired mare down the stable aisle, put her in the biggest stall at the back, and went to the stable door.

"What's next?" I said eagerly.

"I'll get this one myself," Carl said in such a positive voice that I stood humbly to one side as he went back into the van again. I heard a boom and a crash, and then a bright chestnut mare with a lot of white markings came whizzing down the ramp with Carl hanging grimly onto the lead rope.

"She traveled pretty well until about a half hour ago," he said, giving the lead rope a light jerk to make the mare stand still for a moment. "They must have given her a shot of something to load her and keep her quiet on the trip, but the stuff's worn off by now. This mare's supposed to be a children's junior hunter and Russ told me he had a couple of clients looking for a good one, so I brought her along. She's a pretty little thing and fancy enough, but I'd say she's got a few nuts and bolts loose there between the ears."

He shrugged his shoulders and plodded down the stable aisle with the mare dancing and fussing beside him.

"Third stall on the right for her," I said, and went back into the van for the last horse.

The daylight was fading. It was getting late. All I could see of the horse was his tall, dim outline and the narrow white blaze on his face. He was standing quietly and he barely moved as I unsnapped the shipping ties on each side of his halter and unfastened the breastplate across the front of his stall.

"Take it easy with that brown horse," I heard Carl call to me. "He won't give you any trouble, but just watch he doesn't fall down the ramp when you bring him out. He might not be too steady on his legs. I don't know when I've seen a horse in such poor condition."

I let the tall horse take his time as he felt his way down the ramp on his long, thin legs. The lights were on now in the stable, and as I led the horse through the doors, he stopped to look around him.

I glanced at him, waiting, and caught my breath. I couldn't imagine how anyone could let a horse get into such terrible shape. His short brown coat was harsh and dry, pulling across his bones, and his hip joints stuck out as though they were about to poke through his skin. His

4

mane and tail were rough and ragged. One of his shoes was loose and clanked when he moved, and two of his hoofs had no shoes at all. The hoof edges were chipped and uneven.

Carl looked at the horse with his hands on his hips. "Russ is going to have a fit, my bringing a horse in this condition into his barn," he said. "But I didn't know how bad off he was. Some guy upstate called me and said he was closing his stable and only had this one horse left, could I pick it up and peddle it for him. He said the horse was real quiet to ride, and I know a lot of riding-stable owners always looking for quiet hack horses for lessons. So I said sure, I do this all the time. I gave him a couple of hundred bucks and he loaded the horse into the van."

He shook his head disgustedly. "It was very early and still dark, and I was in a hurry to get on down here. Quiet—I'll say he's quiet. Hasn't got hardly enough energy left to stand on his own feet. Looks half dead, doesn't he?"

I thought he looked even more than half dead, but I didn't say so. It had taken me a while, but eventually I'd learned to keep my mouth shut when people were buying and selling horses around me. I stroked the horse's long, bony head gently, but without comment, and Carl sighed and turned away.

"Maybe you could find a stable sheet to throw over him, Abby," he said as I started to lead the horse into a stall. "Cover him up so he doesn't look so bad. I've got to go on with the broodmare tomorrow, but I sure don't want to take that horse with me. I think he'd collapse on the trip. I'll tell Russ I'll pick him up and get him out of here as soon as I can."

I gave the drooping brown horse an extra armload of hay and buckled a green stable sheet on him before I closed his stall door.

"Russ said for you to go down to the house if your van was unloaded before he got back," I said to Carl. "Meg's expecting you for dinner and to spend the night. Don't worry, I'll finish up here for now. I'll be in school tomorrow morning, so you'll be gone by the time I get here in the afternoon. Have a good trip with the broodmare."

Carl gave a grunt of exasperation. "Hope she doesn't go down in the van and start foaling on the New Jersey Turnpike," he said gloomily. "Wonder if that would be a first?"

He gave a farewell wave of his hand and vanished outside the stable door.

The white stable cat came stalking down the aisle followed by her romping litter of six multicolored kittens. We called her Forever, because she was forever having kittens; but she was an excellent mouser and she taught all her kittens to be, too. There was always a waiting list for Forever's kittens, and so her life went on undisturbed in the stable while horses and ponies and people worked around her. It was clear she thought she owned the place and all the animals and people in it.

I fed her in the tack room and went back into the main stable aisle. I loved it when everyone else was gone. I could pretend, for a little while, that all these beautiful horses were mine.

7

I glanced into the stall of the dressage horse that was waiting to fly to Holland. There'd been a mixup with his export papers and he'd been staying over here at High Hickory until everything got straightened out. He was too far from his home in the Southwest to travel all the way back on the van to wait. I didn't go into his stall. Meg and Russ handled this horse themselves.

I didn't always know what happened to all the glorious horses that came through the stable in their travels. High Hickory was only an hour's trip from one of the main airports, and many famous horses came to rest and stay a day or so before they went on their way. Some of them just seemed to disappear. Other times a photograph of one of them would be on the cover of a horse magazine, or the big newspapers would run an article about the horse when it won something fantastic at an international competition. Even though I had little to do with these particular horses, I always felt a bit special at having known them at all. And I often wondered about those we never heard of again.

I checked to see that all the stall latches were tight, turned off the lights inside the stable but left the outside floodlights on for Russ, and rolled the heavy stable door closed behind me.

2

I spun along the darkening back roads toward home. The late spring wind was cold and blew in breathy little gusts. The pale pool of light from my bike bounced around on the road, but I was used to this. I'd found the bike ride home creepy when I'd first started helping out at the High Hickory stables after school. I'd imagined all kinds of sinister things hiding in the woods beside the road, especially in the deep shadows when the dark came earlier and the wind was bitter.

But nothing, not even the shadowy woods or the ice and cold, was going to keep me from the horses.

I'd always liked being with horses and ponies, ever since I could remember. Dad worked for a construction company and we'd moved a number of times. But wherever we'd lived, I'd usually been able to find horses or ponies to work with in all kinds of stables. Some of the stables had been dirty and dark, others were bright and clean, but they all had one thing in common—never enough help. So I was often welcome.

I cleaned stalls and scrubbed and filled water buckets. I walked hot horses and learned how to bandage the legs of lame ones. I cleaned bridles and saddles, washed blankets and shipping bandages, kept quiet and made myself as useful as I knew how. Sometimes I got paid a little and sometimes I didn't. But either way I was sometimes asked to ride and exercise some of the horses and ponies, and that was enough for me.

I watched owners ride and teachers give lessons, tried to sort it all out, and learned scraps about riding wherever I went. Sometimes, if the stables weren't too busy, someone would give me a quick lesson of my own.

Gradually I became known as a "useful" rider, which was a polite way of saying I could stay on a lot of different kinds of horses but didn't look like much. This didn't matter to me, as long as I got to ride at all and be with the horses and ponies.

High Hickory, though, was a whole new world to me. I'd heard of the stables soon after we'd moved into our new house. Meg had grown up nearby. Photographs of her riding show hunters were in the offices of the school building, and she was always asked to present the Sportsmanship Cup at the high-school graduation ceremonies every year.

Two years after she'd graduated herself, she'd been on the Florida horse show circuit where she'd met and married Russ. He was the trainer for a bunch of good show hunters and jumpers for an owner he didn't much like.

Meg and Russ dreamed of having a boarding and showing stable of their own. High Hickory once had been a huge estate, but no one had lived there for years. The main house burned flat one night. While the owners and the town battled over the taxes, the stables on the place were put up for rent. Russ and Meg heard about it and came to lease the little stone gatehouse and the big stables and pastures near the road.

It was a struggle getting started, but the stalls in the big stable were gradually filling with good horses and ponies as the word spread and new clients and pupils came.

The horses and ponies at High Hickory were like none I'd ever known before. From the lesson horses to those belonging to clients, they glowed with quality and good care. The stables were always busy. More good horses came in to be bought or sold, children came for lessons, clients and pupils consulted with Meg and Russ about their horses and showing plans, and always the shining, beautiful horses and ponies were the center of it all.

I'd started by asking if I could help in any way after school and on weekends. They were glad to have me as soon as they saw I knew something about working around horses. At first I scrubbed the water buckets and rolled the bandages and cleaned bridles and saddles and did all the routine chores I could manage.

As time went by I was trusted to do more with the ponies and horses themselves. I helped to lead them in and out of their paddocks for exercise. I helped to hold a fussy horse while the blacksmith made it new shoes and would lend a hand with a frightened pony that didn't like the sound of the electric clipping machine near its ears. And finally the day came when I was asked to ride a very quiet pony whose little owner had chicken pox.

I rode the sweet, furry little thing as though it were as precious as Secretariat, which is what it certainly felt like to me. Meg and Russ both watched every move I made, and I was asked the next day to ride the pony again.

One pony led to another. Meg and Russ had me join their riding lessons whenever it worked out, and I watched and listened and learned every chance I could. The better rider I became, the more they could trust me with the horses and ponies in their care. I was no longer content to be a "useful" rider. I wanted to be a good one.

I shivered and shifted the grip of my cold hands on the handlebars of my bicycle. As usual, I'd forgotten to wear my gloves.

All my life I'd wanted a horse or a pony of my own. This was always out of the question—horses and ponies of any kind were much too expensive to buy and keep. But my dreams and daydreams had always been pleasantly vague. I'd picture horses running free in a field with their manes and tails flying in the wind, or see a van go by on the highway and catch a quick glimpse of a horse turning its head toward me, and I'd want them, any of them, for my own.

But none of these dream horses would do any more. I wanted a *good* horse, and this made the dream more impossible than ever. But just as much fun to think about.

In the meantime, at least I was with good horses at High Hickory. As I pedaled around the potholes in the road left by the spring thaw, I wondered if the Thoroughbred mare would have her foal during the night. What excitement there would be in the morning. The squirrely chestnut mare wouldn't stay at the stables long, I knew, and I had no idea at all what was under the fuzzy polar bear coat of the gray Connemara pony other than a pair of large, dark, kind eyes. And the poor thin brown horse with the long black legs—at least he'd get decent feed for a while, and a clean, comfortable stall to sleep in.

I bumped my bike up our driveway and hurried thankfully into the warmth of the house.

"You're late." My sister, Ellie, who was two years older than I was and a junior in high school, called to me from the living room. I took off my jacket and followed the sound of her voice, which I could barely hear over the screaming game show she was watching on television.

"I told Mom I'd be later than usual this evening," I said, turning the sound on the set down. "I had to wait for some new horses to come in."

"Horses," said Ellie. "Don't they ever get to be a bore? Mom and Dad have gone to a fund-raising meeting for the new library wing. There's meat loaf in the oven for your supper."

She shook her long blonde hair back away from her face and looked at her fingernails critically. "Do you like this new color? It's called 'Sunbeams.' "

"It's pretty," I said. I glanced down at my own hands, which were cold and dusty, and shoved them into the pockets of my jeans. Ellie always looked pretty. She was tall, and smart, and the president of her class. I often wished I were more like Ellie and that I looked like her, too, with her beautiful hair. Mine was a nothing kind of dark blonde. It tangled itself unevenly in the wind and when I wore my hard hunt cap out riding, so I kept it short. That didn't help much. It just got wispy instead.

Ellie had kind of smoky gray eyes, and mine were just a plain, ordinary blue. But if I was short and kind of square, there sure wasn't much use in wasting time brooding about it.

I smiled at her. "You won't think the polish is so nice if it spills all over the couch," I told her. "It looks as though the bottle's tipping. I know I'm late, but can you still help me a little with my math homework tonight?"

"Sure," Ellie said. "You'd better get yourself some supper first, though. You must be starved."

I was hungry. And I was tired, too. It had been a long day, but I still had to battle through my homework before I could even think of going to bed. Mom and Dad didn't mind my spending a lot of time riding at High Hickory as long as my schoolwork got done and my marks didn't go down, so I worked hard to keep it all together. I wasn't going to let *anything* keep me from the horses.

3

The sun was bright, and the whole world seemed to smell of spring as I swung off the school bus the next afternoon. I ran into the house, grabbed my hard black hunt cap from the closet and a handful of Fig Newtons from the kitchen, and rode my bike over to High Hickory.

The willow trees near the ponds were softening into a blurry lemony yellow, the tiny new leaves on the maples were a deep red, and there were musical chirpings and tiny singing sounds near the streams and ponds. The dry winter grass had lost its dreary look and was washed over with pale green. Even the New England stone walls, which had looked so bleak and cold all winter, were a prettier gray in the spring sunlight, and pink and white dogwood trees shone like starlight deep in the woods.

I whistled happily as I put my bike away. Meg and Russ had a fit if anyone left a bicycle out near the stables, where a shying horse might tangle in it. I put it carefully in a shed and went into the stable.

Donna, who had been stable manager for Meg and Russ right from the beginnings of High Hickory, was sweeping the stable aisle as I came in the door.

"Hi, Abby," she said. "Russ has been looking for you."

Russ came out of the stable office just then. "Abby, the Richmonds are coming this afternoon to look at the gray Connemara that came in yesterday. Would you get up on him for me and take him out to the ring? I'd like to see what kind of a pony he is before the Richmonds get here."

"Sure," I said. Wonderful. I'd expected to be cleaning tack most of the afternoon, but I'd much rather ride.

I asked about the broodmare and was disappointed to hear that she'd not had her foal during the night. Carl had driven his van off early in the morning, still unhappily predicting she'd lie down and go into labor while he was on the turnpike with her.

"He promised he'd call tonight and let us know," said Donna. She led the pony out of his stall, and I shook my head wonderingly. His furry polar bear coat was gone. He was smooth and sleek from being clipped that morning, and his mane and tail had been washed and trimmed. He was a very handsome pony.

Donna left him cross-tied in the aisle and went to get a saddle and bridle. I started to follow to help.

"Wait, Abby," Russ said. "Would you take that ugly brown horse out first? Put him in the back field. I don't want any of my clients to see him. I don't want anyone thinking he's an example of how we care for our horses here. He'd give any stable a bad name, looking the way he does."

I patted the horse sympathetically and put a halter on his bony head. Donna stopped by the open stall door with her arms full of tack as I fastened the buckles.

"I can't understand why anybody would let a horse get into that kind of shape," she said sadly. "He hasn't got swamp fever, either. Meg checked his shipping papers the minute she saw him. Of course, the certificate could be faked. The vet's already been here to do another Coggins test on him just to make sure. His teeth are okay and he seems to be basically all right. It just looks as though he hasn't had enough to eat for quite a while."

The horse followed me slowly as I led him down the lane between the paddocks. I went through the gate that led into the big back pasture and unsnapped the lead rope. He wandered off quietly, raising his head just for a moment to look around him before he buried his muzzle in the rich spring grass.

I latched the gate, looped the lead rope over a fence post, and ran back to the stables.

The Connemara was kind and cheerful. He did everything he was asked to do in the muddy ring and then jumped four nice jumps when Russ told me to try them.

Russ looked pleased as I pulled up to a walk and patted the pony's neck. "This may be just right for the Richmond boy," he said. "I've known the pony for a few years and he's just the ticket, I think. Get him back to Donna and we'll get the mud off him and brush him off some before the Richmonds get here. They should be here soon. You haven't seen Angela today, have you, Abby? She's supposed to ride the pony for them this afternoon so they can watch him go."

"Nope. Sorry." I pulled my hunt cap farther down

over my eyes and made a face Russ couldn't see. Angela Welles was a pain. To me, anyway. She had a super beautiful horse of her own named Wayfarer that she kept here at High Hickory. She rode a lot in horse shows and she won a lot, too. She'd even won a ribbon last fall at the show at Madison Square Garden in New York.

Angela was a smooth, polished rider and rode the best of the High Hickory ponies and horses when prospective clients came to see them. I struggled to learn to ride the way she did, but I was usually put up on the rougher, more unschooled horses while she got to ride the fancy ones to show them of.

I ran the stirrup irons up on the leathers and started back to the stable. "If Angela isn't here in time, would you ride this pony for the Richmonds?" Russ called after me.

"Okay." I pushed my cap up, back where it belonged, and wished Angela two flat tires and a broken axle on the car, wherever she was, so she couldn't get here in time to ride. I delivered the Connemara into Donna's waiting hands and hurried to the tack room to tidy up.

My faded denim jacket and lumpy gray sweater looked too shabby for showing a pony to a client. I took off my jacket, found a down vest someone had left on a hook, and put it on. It wasn't leaking too many feathers, and I looked a little better. I did my best to shove my wispy hair back under my cap. I wiped the mud off my paddock boots, brushed what I could off my jeans, and sighed as I looked at myself in the tack room mirror. Hardly the elegant Angela Welles, but the best I could do.

18

I went back to wait nervously by the stable door. My heart sank when I heard the sound of a car in the stable drive, but it wasn't Angela's mother rushing her daughter to ride—it was the Richmonds, a little bit early.

Mrs. Richmond and her son, Tommy, went to speak to Russ. I waved to Tommy. I didn't know him well, but we went to the same school and I'd seen him at some of the soccer and baseball games.

Russ nodded to me. I spun around and tore down the aisle to get the gray pony. Donna gave me a ferocious look—it was stupid to run in a stable. I slowed down guiltily, took the pony's reins, and grinned at Donna. No matter what, it was too late for Angela now. It was my turn.

4

The pony went along nicely. I concentrated carefully, trying to remember everything Meg had taught me during all my lessons, and I rode as smoothly as I knew how.

I liked the pony more every minute of the ride and we had a great time together, doing everything Russ asked us to do while Mrs. Richmond watched and smiled, and Tommy looked bored.

Mrs. Richmond had a horse of her own, a silly-headed but well-bred gray Thoroughbred mare named Azalea, which she boarded here at High Hickory. All of us knew that Tommy had been in a bad car accident the past winter, when it slid on an icy road on the way to a basketball game. One of his legs had been badly crushed. His limp was barely noticeable, but he could no longer play soccer or the other sports he'd liked so much.

Mrs. Richmond had always loved horses and riding, and was hoping Tommy might learn to enjoy them, too. He was taking riding lessons from Meg, but his heart wasn't in it. Mrs. Richmond thought he might like riding more if he had a good, dependable horse or pony of his own. Meg and Russ had been looking for some time for just the right one.

Russ nodded to me. I rode into the center of the ring and stopped.

"Thank you, Abby," Russ said. I got off and stood there happily in the spring mud while Russ put Tommy up in the saddle, adjusted the stirrups, and sent him off to try the pony himself. As Tommy rode toward the ring rail, Russ dropped his voice.

"Now get that brown horse away from here, Abby," he said. "You must have left the pasture gate open."

"But I never . . ." I started to say, but Russ just gave me a cold look and turned to speak to Mrs. Richmond.

Almost unbelieving, I looked behind me. The scrawny brown horse was there all right, grazing peacefully just outside the ring.

My face burned with embarrassment. Leaving a pasture gate unlatched was a very careless thing to do. As quickly and quietly as possible, I slid through the ring rails and went over to the horse. He let me catch him by the halter without any trouble, and I led him again down the lane between the paddocks, expecting to see the wide field gate swinging open on its hinges. But it wasn't. The gate was firmly in place, and the latch was tight.

I shrugged my shoulders. I supposed the opened gate could have swung shut behind the horse after he'd escaped. Probably I'd been in too much of a hurry to fasten the latch properly. It could have snapped back into place when the gate swung shut.

I put the horse back into the field, and this time I took the lead rope from where I'd left it on the post and knotted it around the latch.

The horse walked off into the pasture, grazing, and I started back to the stables.

I was only halfway down the lane when I heard the sound of soft hoofbeats behind me. I whirled around, startled, and saw the brown horse jogging slowly toward me.

He stopped patiently when I said "Whoa." I grabbed his halter again and towed him grimly back to the gate. The knotted rope was still in place and the gate was safely shut. I opened everything up, put the horse back into the field, and retied the rope around the closed latch.

"This is getting to be a silly bore. Let alone the fact you're getting me into trouble," I told the horse crossly.

I set out to check all the fencing, including the hidden places where it dipped behind the hill. But there wasn't a rail down anywhere. I walked every inch of the fence, which seemed endless. I got hot in the down vest and took it off, trudging wearily back up the hill.

The thin brown horse with his incredibly long black legs was still grazing peacefully where I'd left him in the field. He didn't look as though he had enough energy to move more than a step or two at a time.

"No more of this," I said to him as I went by. "You're wearing *me* out, whatever you're up to."

I started the trip back to the stables again. But instead of going the whole way, I hid behind a thick bunch of bushes just leafing out beside the lane and waited, watching the pasture gate through the branches.

Sure enough. A few minutes later I saw the horse raise his head, look around him, and jog slowly toward the

gate. He was barely moving, but he floated over the gate like a silent shadow.

Again he stopped when I said "Whoa." I was tired of it all. I'd tramped up and down that lane with the darned horse what had begun to seem like a dozen times. I tugged the horse over nearer the lane fence, climbed to the top rail, and wiggled onto his sharp, thin back.

"If you've got enough strength to jump the way you just did, then you can carry me back to the stables this time," I told him. With one hand on the back of his halter, I guided him at a walk the rest of the way to the stable yard.

"But that gate's got to be at least five feet high," said Donna as I put the horse away in his stall and buckled a stable sheet on him. He sipped at the water in the stall bucket and started to eat his hay.

"Maybe so," I said. "But it sure didn't stop him. You should have seen him jump it. No problem."

As it turned out, she had lots of chances to see him do it. So did Meg and Russ, who had a hard time believing me at first. But within a few days there wasn't a fence or a gate on the place the brown horse hadn't jumped on his own. And when Russ himself put the horse in the stallion paddock, behind a six-and-a-half-foot board fence, only to watch him walk across the paddock and jump out the other side, we all gave up.

Quiet, half starved as he was, this horse wanted to do things his own way. He wandered around the place as he

24

pleased, jumping from paddock to paddock whenever he liked. We kept a stable sheet on him to make him look more presentable, because he wouldn't stay discreetly out of sight in a back field, hiding his pitiful bones.

All of us were sorry for him. I often brought carrots and apples for him. Donna brushed him off and combed the tangles out of his mane and tail, and Meg and Russ gave him all the grain he could manage without making him sick. But there wasn't anything more we could do for him except feed him well, turn him out to pasture every day, and let him gain the weight he needed so badly.

"He might be worth keeping around for a while," Russ said as we watched the horse jump the pasture fence into the lane and start grazing again. "Hard to tell with a horse like this."

Carl had called from Pennsylvania to tell us the bay mare had a nice black colt, born less than an hour after he'd put her away in her new stall. He told Russ he'd be back in a few days to pick up the dizzy little chestnut mare and the brown horse to take them away.

But by the time Carl stopped by with his van on his return trip from Pennsylvania, Russ had made up his mind. He paid Carl for the brown horse. He'd finally decided to give him a while longer to see what time, along with good feed and care, might do for the strange, dark horse.

5

The vet checked the gray Connemara and passed him with flying colors as sound. Mrs. Richmond bought him, though Tommy didn't seem to care much one way or the other. The vet went over the brown horse again, ran several more blood tests, and could find nothing wrong.

"He certainly isn't sick," he told Meg and Russ when he called with the results of the tests a few days later. "It still has all the looks of plain starvation, as far as I've been able to tell. Give him time and feed him up. I'll bring a vitamin-mineral supplement for him the next time I come by your place."

The blacksmith trimmed and shod the horse's neglected hoofs. Everybody in the stable tried to think of a name for him, and we finally settled on Sandpiper. With his long skinny black legs, he did look like the quick little dark birds that ran along the edges of the sea.

Tommy named his pony Shamrock because, he told me, the Connemaras were a small, rugged breed of horses from the west coast of Ireland. Some Connemaras, like Arabians, were no taller than the horse show height measurement that divided horses from ponies. But, like Arabians, they were really small horses.

26

New clients came to High Hickory with their horses. Old clients suddenly wanted new ones. More young riders came for lessons as the weather brightened and grew warmer. Horses and ponies that hadn't been worked or schooled much during the winter were put on the routine exercising list again.

There were new people helping Donna. They washed and trimmed and clipped and brought out lightweight blankets and sheets from the storage trunks. The clippers whirled endlessly and vans drove in and out, all to the accompaniment of the busy blacksmith's anvil.

I rode and rode every day after school. The saddle I used never seemed to cool off as it went from one horse to another. There were small local schooling shows almost every weekend, and when Meg took a vanload of horses and ponies and small pupils, I went along to help. I shortened stirrups, straightened reins, chased after missing numbers, and congratulated the riders who won ribbons and comforted those who didn't.

Angela Welles never came to the schooling shows. She and her lovely Wayfarer only went to the big ones. So I was the one who did the practice schooling on reluctant or fresh horses and ponies, and sometimes I was asked to ride one of them in its first few classes. This was fun, and I looked forward to the horse show weekends.

Mrs. Richmond came by one of the shows one day, watched me for a while, and asked Meg if I could show Shamrock the next weekend to see how well he might do in pony hunter classes. Meg told me about it as we were going home that afternoon in the van. "Mrs. Richmond knows you like the pony and you look well on him. Would you like to ride him through an entire show?"

I was very nearly speechless with delight. "Sure. I'd like to. Very much," I said.

Meg shifted gears to turn through the stable gates. "Good. I thought you might. It seems to me Mrs. Richmond might be hoping that if the pony does well enough, Tommy could become interested in showing him a few times this summer."

I didn't think so, but it was none of my business.

I was awake practically the whole night before the show, listening to rain pouring outside in the dark, worrying that the show might be canceled. But by dawn the rain had stopped. The storm was breaking up and blowing away as Meg drove the van onto the soggy horse show grounds the next morning.

I had borrowed a coat that didn't quite fit but that looked well enough to get by at a schooling show, used clouds of spray to keep my hair back under my hunt cap, and polished my boots until they glittered.

The damp fields steamed as the sun rose higher, and the mist, fragrant with spring, mixed with the smells of liniment, horses, polished leather, and crushed grass. It was a wonderful smell, and I breathed it in with excitement as I grinned at Meg and went to get Shamrock from the van.

It seemed strange to be the one fussed over a little. For the first time it was my own boots that were not supposed to get muddy and my show clothes that were supposed to be kept clean. Someone else got Shamrock's number for me and helped tie it around my waist. My insides were shaking, which was a most peculiar feeling, and I was glad I hadn't eaten any breakfast. I just hoped my nervousness didn't show.

Shamrock was his usual sensible self. He looked an awful lot calmer than I felt.

"Take your time." Meg was talking to me, and I struggled to bring her into focus. "Walk the pony around and let him get used to things. I don't know if he's ever been to a show before, and we don't want to surprise him with too much that's new. Let him hear the loudspeakers up close and walk him around the course. The committee isn't allowing any practice schooling over the fences because of all the mud, but you can let him see the jumps anyway."

I nodded without speaking, somehow got my reins together, and Shamrock and I drifted around the show grounds. We inspected the flags that marked the course and went up to each jump to have a good look at it. None of them looked threatening or difficult.

The loudspeakers crackled and hummed. This didn't bother Shamrock, either. At a signal from Meg I started to warm up at a trot and a canter.

"No problems," I reported to Meg as I rode over to her. "Shamrock's fine."

Meg nodded approvingly. "Do you know you've got the first class? Large ponies go first and then they'll lower the fences for the medium and small ponies. Have you checked out the course?"

My face went hot. I'd forgotten. I'd looked at each individual fence, but I hadn't remembered to check the order in which they were to be jumped.

I turned Shamrock quickly and jogged over to the post near the start of the course, where there was a diagram marked on a big white card. It was a simple course, but it started over the first jump to the left and not to the right, as I had supposed it would. I patted Shamrock guiltily as I memorized the course.

"Okay?" said Meg a few minutes later. "You're listed third in the large pony jumping order. You'd better get over to the starter to let him know you're on deck."

I sat on Shamrock like a lump and watched the first two ponies go over the course. The first pony stopped at almost every jump and the second one didn't want to start at all. Once his rider and trainer got him going, though, he jumped well.

"Ready?" said Meg. "They're calling your number. On your way, now," and she gave Shamrock a friendly slap on his hindquarters.

I'd have liked to believe it was my spectacular riding that made Shamrock jump so well. But all I really did was cluck to him, set him into a canter when his number was called, and guide him toward the first fence of the course. He carried me around, jumping carefully and well in spite of the thick, sticky mud, and Meg looked pleased as I pulled up at the finish and trotted toward her.

"Good trip," she said. I patted Shamrock and swung off his back. I ran the stirrups up, loosened the girth, and walked him away from the crowd of ponies waiting their turn to go. Shamrock chinked his bit and the course flags snapped in the rising wind. A horse whinnied inside a trailer and another one answered. My insides had stopped shaking and at last I was able to breathe again without gulping for air. I smiled to myself and rubbed Shamrock's soft muzzle gratefully.

Shamrock won the class. The ringmaster put the blue ribbon on his bridle and handed me a little silver bowl. I murmured a thank you—I wasn't sure what else I was supposed to do, but it seemed to be the right thing—and led Shamrock over to where Meg was waiting.

"That's nice," she said. "Good pony, and you rode him well."

It was a wonderful day. The blue ribbon fluttered cheerfully where it was hung on the side of the van ramp, and it was even nicer when another blue and then a red ribbon for the second place we won in a walk, trot and canter class were hung beside it.

"Shamrock's not the fanciest mover in the world," Meg said appraisingly as I started to wrap Shamrock's legs for the trip home. "But he certainly is a good, honest jumper. I wouldn't bother with the leg wraps yet, Abby. Championships are awarded by points, and Shamrock has done well."

Sure enough, the announcer's voice came over the loudspeaker calling the pony's number. I led him into the ring for the blue, red, and yellow championship ribbon. I was beaming like an idiot by then, but I couldn't pretend any longer that I wasn't thrilled by it all.

6

Mrs. Richmond was pleased and Tommy pretended to be as I gave them their bright ribbons and silver cups at the stable the next time they came.

"I think you should keep them, Abby," Mrs. Richmond said, but Meg, who also was there, shook her head.

"The ribbons belong to the pony," she said with a smile. "Abby did a nice job of riding him, but Shamrock won the ribbons and the trophies."

"Big deal," I heard Tommy say under his breath as he went to put the ribbons in the car. I followed him outside. He'd dropped the championship ribbon with its long streamers in the stable aisle and I took it to the car.

"I know it wasn't exactly the National Horse Show," I said, annoyed, as I caught up with him. "But still. Aren't you glad for Shamrock?"

He took the championship ribbon I gave him and tossed it onto the front seat of the car with the others. Their bright colors shimmered in the sunlight and sparks of silver twinkled on the curved rims of the trophies.

"I already *know* he's a nice pony," said Tommy. "I don't need ribbons and stuff to tell me that. I just don't think it's all that exciting, that's all."

I shrugged my shoulders and went back to the stable. Poor Mrs. Richmond didn't seem to be getting very far in trying to get Tommy interested in doing much with Shamrock.

We tried once more. Mrs. Richmond arranged with Meg for me to ride Shamrock in another show the following week. There were more good ponies showing that day, and some of them were beautiful and very smooth. Shamrock and I didn't sweep all before us, as we had the week before. This was mostly my fault, at least in the first class. When they called Shamrock's number my mind had been wandering—I'd been watching a young horse playing as he was being exercised—and so I bustled Shamrock into an unsteady canter toward the first brush jump.

He jumped it well enough, but the approach had been ragged, and I felt disorganized all through the course. Meg was not pleased. Neither was I, especially since I felt I'd cheated Shamrock out of the higher ribbon he deserved.

We got a pink ribbon for fifth place. I accepted it from the ringmaster with a polite smile and wanted to bury it deep in my pocket, where it could lie forgotten in a dark spot. But Meg insisted on hanging it on the van ramp wing as always. Everywhere I went on the show grounds that day it seemed I could see that rotten ribbon twinkling at me from the ramp.

When I went to get Shamrock ready for his next class, Meg held his reins quietly while I checked the tightness of the girth before getting on.

"Let it be," Meg said as I reached for the reins. "That last class is over. Relax. I'm not telling you to forget it. Just file it in the back of your mind. When you're out there before a class, remember what you're there for. I can't ride the pony from the ground. You're the one in charge. Keep your mind on your job. And now quit hassling yourself, or you'll never get a smooth ride."

This time I was so alert for my turn to be called that I felt like a stick as I broke Shamrock into a canter. He set his jaw stiffly against the bit, which he never had done before, resenting the tenseness in my hands. I forced myself deliberately to suck in a deep breath and to uncurl my rigid fingers that had been clutching the reins. Shamrock reached out in a longer stride, more comfortable at last, and pricked his gray ears knowingly at the first jump.

"Okay," I said under my breath as we landed after a beautiful jump, and Shamrock swung on toward the next jump, a white gate, without changing the easy cadence of his gallop.

It was a much better round over the course, steady and consistent. I pulled Shamrock up, feeling a lot better.

"Nice," said Meg as I rode over to her. "That was an even, trustworthy children's hunter kind of way to go. Never mind the placings. There are some very good ponies here today, and some of them have gone well. All you need to know is that you gave a good ride to a good pony."

He was second this time, to a handsome bay pony with white socks who jumped well and was a better mover than Shamrock. Both Meg and I were perfectly happy with the red ribbon on Shamrock's bridle.

The day stretched out until the vans and the fences began to throw deep shadows. There were horses and ponies jamming the rings and courses in every class. Shamrock had been entered in two divisions, pony hunters and children's hunters, and by the time twilight fell and we wearily started for home in the van, he'd won a heap of ribbons, a few trophies, and was reserve champion pony hunter to the bay pony, who had been champion.

"You never know with these schooling shows," said Meg as she turned the van carefully into the driveway of High Hickory. "Sometimes there's only a handful of ponies and horses, and other times all the stables in the area come out. That's sure what it looked like today. It was a good show, Abby. You rode well."

I nodded, content. And I'd learned a lot, too.

Again Mrs. Richmond accepted the ribbons and trophies with a smile and again Tommy couldn't have cared less.

I looked forward with excitement to the next weekend's showing, but Meg told me a few days later that Mrs. Richmond wasn't planning to send Shamrock out showing again.

"She never bought that pony to try to win a trunkful of ribbons," said Meg. "He's not fancy enough for the bigger shows, and she knows this. She only hoped Tommy might find it fun. And since it doesn't matter to him, there's no use going on with it."

36

I stared at her with a stricken look. "I'm sorry," said Meg. "I know you enjoyed it. We'll find you something else to show some day soon. There's bound to be a horse or a pony coming in that needs to get out in a schooling show or two."

I went sadly to Shamrock's stall and gave him the apple I'd brought for him. I tried not to grow too fond of the ponies or horses I rode, because they were never mine and I never knew how long they'd be at High Hickory. Many came in to the stable and went on again, sometimes without my even knowing they were on their way until I saw a name missing from the exercise list.

But I'd always liked Shamrock, right from the first, and I'd started to worry about him. If Tommy didn't get any kind of kick out of riding, I knew in my bones that the pony would not stay. I felt a sharp pang in my stomach that I told myself was the piece of apple I'd bitten off and eaten before giving the rest to Shamrock, but as I turned from his stall, I sighed regretfully. I knew very well it wasn't the bite of apple on an empty stomach. Not having a horse or a pony of my own was a pain.

Tough. But there it was. I checked the latch on Shamrock's door and went to help Donna with a young horse that was giving her a hard time.

7

There was another show scheduled for Saturday, and the weather forecast was for a clear, bright day. Suddenly it seemed that every client at High Hickory wanted to go. Meg asked me to go to help, and of course I said I would; but it was awful to pull on jeans instead of my showing breeches early Saturday morning. I crammed my breeches, boots, and borrowed jacket into a zippered bag to take along, just in case somebody important suddenly ran up to me at the show needing a rider. But all this got me was a wobbling ride on my bike to the stables with the bag hanging unevenly on the handlebars.

I threw my bag in with the tack trunks just as the last horse was loaded into the van—and that's just where it was, undisturbed, at the end of the day.

The show was an absolute zoo. The parking area was jammed with vans and trailers. Little ponies with screaming kids on their backs zipped in and out like mosquitoes. Young horses spun and danced, others whinnied to their stablemates. A gray horse fell backwards out of the trailer next to our van, nearly squashing its frantic owner, who seemed more concerned about the grass stains now on the horse than the cut on its leg.

Meg went to soothe the owner and send for the show

vet. It turned out he hadn't arrived yet, so she patched up the horse with our first-aid kit while Donna and I got our own crew ready.

We walked hot horses, soothed excited riders, and loaded and unloaded horses and ponies in and out of the vans between their classes until my head was spinning. I felt I'd spent the day with a sponge in one hand and a sweat scraper in the other, when I wasn't rolling up shipping bandages, catching loose ponies and trying to find their owners, or searching wildly for one of our own riders due in the ring on a horse I was holding. But almost everyone had a good time. The horses and ponies won their share of ribbons, and our van ramp wings were bright with ribbons of all the horse show colors with a championship or two by the end of the long, busy day.

The last little rider was scooped up by its parents. The last of the ribbons were claimed by the happy owners, and the last of the daylight was fading as we started home. Meg thanked me for my help as she moved the van slowly across the rough ground of the parking area toward the road.

"I like doing this," I said. "You know I like working with the horses and ponies—all of it."

Meg smiled. "But you'd rather be riding. I know."

Just ahead of us a twelve-horse van was backing up at an angle to make the turn onto the narrow back road. As we waited, Meg stretched and pushed her hair back from her hot face. "Long day," she said. "These schooling shows can be wild. Never mind, Abby, you're just getting started. You'll get your chance."

The huge van in front of us finally made its way out of

the field, and we followed it onto the road.

We still had the horses and ponies to unload and unbraid. Russ had rushed off with a client to catch a plane to Michigan to look at a horse, so Donna, Meg, and I unwrapped the shipping bandages, sponged off the horses and a pony that had broken out into a sweat on the trip home, and walked them until they were dry and cool.

The fragrance of leg brace drifted through the stable aisles. Fireflies began to spark in the darkening pastures. Forever came out to sit on the mounting block in the shadows beside the stable door, watching the fireflies as the horse I was cooling off grazed at the end of the lead rope. I whistled contentedly under my breath. After the frenzy of a busy show, I loved this time of day. Tired as we all were, it was good to unwind as we made the horses comfortable and put them away for the night.

Our first big show of the season swept down on us just as school was ending for the summer. Angela Welles and her beautiful Wayfarer were entered and, of course, I wanted to go along. Meg said I'd be welcome to help with Wayfarer during the show.

Angela and I compared notes, ducked end-of-the-year class meetings, shuffled our schedules however we could, somehow got through our final exams, and met triumphantly at High Hickory the first morning of the show.

It seemed funny to be going to a horse show on a weekday, but the big ones were all five or six days long. The Hunt Club grounds weren't far, and Angela's first class wasn't until after ten o'clock. Even so, we left early so there'd be no pressure in getting the horse and his rider ready to go into the ring.

40

Stabling tents covered fields and paddocks for those horses coming from a long distance. However, Russ and Meg preferred to have their horses stay at High Hickory at night when the show grounds weren't too far away and the vanning trip wasn't too long and tiring for them.

There were three show rings rimmed with fresh white board fences and an outside course well away from the rings that stretched out invitingly between white and red flags. There were huge schooling and exercising areas. Loudspeakers and bright banners were everywhere, and gold- and white-striped tenting over the spectator stands and boxes.

I tried to see it all at once out of the van window while Meg went through the papers and formalities at the entrance to the grounds. Eventually official passes were given to her, and we rolled slowly past the stabling area and found the proper place to leave the van.

Wayfarer stepped down the van ramp with a wise look. He certainly knew what showing was all about. His mane had been put up in a row of tiny braids that made his lovely head and neck look more handsome than ever. The top part of his tail was braided, and he had been groomed and polished until he glowed.

I set to work unwrapping the shipping bandages from his legs while Meg and Angela went off to get numbers and check rings and courses. As I worked, I glanced around me over my shoulder. I watched other horses being unloaded and gotten ready by their grooms. Except for the sound of hoofs on the van ramps and an occasional word from a groom to a fussy horse, it was quiet. Voices were low and faces were unsmiling and intense. "Heavy scene, this big-show stuff," I said to Wayfarer under my breath. He lowered his head and nuzzled my arm with gentle dignity.

Meg had helped me carry Angela's gleaming lacquered tack trunk down from the van. Its protective canvas covering had been taken off. Wayfarer's dark and polished show bridle was there, and I put it on him with fussy care, making sure all the buckles were lying flat and even and every strap was tucked firmly into its leather keeper. There was another box full of grooming equipment. I wiped Wayfarer off with a soft linen cloth and carefully put his saddle on.

Meg and Angela came back, discussing the course for the first class. Angela swung gracefully into the saddle and rode off quietly on her horse while Meg told me what to bring out to the ring—hoof oil, white cornstarch powder, a brush, two or three clean linen cloths, hoofpick, and a dampened sponge. We put all this into another, smaller box with a handle. Meg shook out a soft blanket the color of cream that had Angela's initials on it in dark red. She folded it over her arm, picked up a light, open-weave sheet in matching colors, and we went out onto the show grounds.

Beautiful horses were everywhere, being walked or warmed up at a gentle trot on the brilliant green grass of the field. Some horses were being worked by their trainers, each circling at the end of a long line. A few were being led with the wide coolers over their backs rippling as they moved. There was the scent of coffee from the refreshment stand, where a few riders and trainers huddled, speaking in low voices. And, above it all, the sweet smell of grass lightly crushed by horses' hoofs.

8

The announcer called the first of Angela's classes. The judges walked into the ring. Angela brought Wayfarer over to me and I dusted cornstarch on the white socks above his hoofs, wiped off the specks that had drifted onto the dark markings of his legs, and brushed on the hoof oil, careful not to get any of the stain on his socks. I took the bandage off his tail that was there to keep the braiding smoothly in place when the horse wasn't in the ring. Meg rubbed the horse's bit with a clean cloth to bring up every spark of shine while Angela pulled on her gloves and smoothed them on her hands.

Another clean cloth wiped off Angela's black boots, and then the stirrup irons were given a last polish. Meg checked Wayfarer's bridle with swift, expert hands and eyes to make sure the horse was comfortable and that everything was right. The tightness of the girth was checked for a second time, and Meg finally nodded her approval.

Angela tugged down her coat, reset her feet in the stirrups, and nodded back to Meg. The wide white gate to the ring swung open and the first rider's number was called.

There were almost fifty horses and riders in every one of Angela's classes. I watched the grooms as the first horses ended their jumping rounds and trotted from the ring, one at a time, and so I was ready and knew what to do when Angela rode Wayfarer out.

I was right there to take the horse's reins as she slipped out of the saddle and hurried over to Meg to discuss her performance and watch the other competitors ride. I threw Wayfarer's cooler over his warm back and led him away from the gate. I loosened his girth but left his saddle on under the cooler, as everyone else was doing, and walked him quietly until his breathing was normal. I brushed the dust from his legs, smoothed his coat with a cloth, and rubbed the bridle and saddle leather until they were spotless again.

I could have asked Meg about all the things I was supposed to do, but it all made sense as I watched how the other horses were being cared for. I had no idea if Wayfarer's part of this class was over, but nobody else seemed to be taking their horses back to the stabling area, so I stayed put. When I saw the white powders and hoof oils coming out of their boxes around me, I did the same, and Wayfarer looked terrific when Angela suddenly rushed over to get him.

"Girth," I said swiftly to remind her to check it. I should have remembered to do this myself. She gave me a quick, nervous smile as a thank you, tightened the loosened girth as I pulled off Wayfarer's wide cooler, and jogged her horse back into the ring.

Eventually I got the different classes sorted out. In equitation classes each rider jumped the course and was judged on horsemanship alone. It wasn't hard, though, to tell that a horse of quality and smooth elegance, like Wayfarer, made a big difference in how its rider looked to the judges. Sometimes a few riders were asked to jump again over a changed course, and sometimes they went back to ride at a walk, trot, and canter. It looked very boring to me, but it seemed to matter a lot to the trainers and riders who were there.

I found the junior hunter classes easier to understand, since I'd ridden in some of them in schooling shows. In these classes the horse itself counted—the smooth way it moved, and the evenness and quality of its jumping ability.

I didn't get to see many of the other horses go. I was kept busy with Wayfarer and I gave up trying to keep track of who won what.

The day grew hotter, and the horse needed sponging off between classes. The warm cooler was replaced by the open weave of the light sheet and a little fly repellent was smoothed onto his coat.

"You were wonderful today," Meg said as we drove home that afternoon. "You didn't say much, though. Did you enjoy the show?"

"I was too busy to talk," I said with a laugh. "Wow. I never saw so many horses turned out in such perfection. And those were all kids' horses."

Meg smiled. "It doesn't make any difference. Not any more. The quality of competition in the big shows today is fierce, the horses are splendid, and every tiniest detail must be perfection. Or forget it. No room for middle ground at these shows."

She moved her shoulders stiffly. "I don't really know

which is tougher for a trainer, taking fifteen little ones to a schooling show or managing one horse and rider under this kind of pressure at these big shows."

Angela had gone home with a friend. When we got back to the stable, I helped take the braids out of Wayfarer's mane with Donna fussing over my shoulder.

"Careful now, Abby," she said at least a million times. "Just cut the braiding threads, not one hair of that mane, okay? We can't have a cut mane that looks like a toothbrush by the end of the show season."

She unbraided the horse's tail herself and smoothed the wavy hair with a damp brush.

"Doesn't he go back to the show again tomorrow?" I said. "Why can't you leave the mane and tail braided?"

Donna looked horrified. "The hair would break, and he might even start to rub his mane during the night. That's murder. It does an awful lot of damage to the hair. Don't worry about it, I'll put it up again in the morning."

I knew what that meant. Donna would be braiding Wayfarer again long before daylight.

"Sure makes a long day," I said.

"Just part of the ball game," Donna said cheerfully. She knelt to hand-rub Wayfarer's legs with rubbing alcohol, and I went to get fresh sheets of cotton and some flannel bandages for her. The horse was groomed lightly again, his stable sheet buckled in place, and his legs done up in supporting bandages before he was finally put away in his stall.

9

The schedule of classes was much lighter the next day. Wayfarer even had the chance to go back to the van and stay in his stall for a while between classes, happily pulling wisps of hay from the stuffed hay net hung high on the van partition, where he could reach it comfortably. Meg said she'd stay by the van to keep an eye on him, and this gave me a chance to watch some of the other classes in the show.

I'd seen enough equitation and junior hunters to last me a while, so I went to the main ring to watch a class of junior jumpers. I expected something different from what Angela and Wayfarer had been doing, but I had no idea what a "jumper" class meant.

The jumps looked enormous. They were much higher than the hunter class jumps and were set in crazy patterns, zigzagging all over the ring at different angles. I hung onto the ring fence with excitement as I watched the horses take their turns over the course.

These weren't the pretty horses and slickly smooth riders of the equitation or hunter classes. Some of the horses even looked like ordinary, everyday horses, and many of them were unbraided. But they all were incredible jumpers.

The classes were judged only on the mistakes a horse made, if any were made at all. Touching a fence as it was jumped or knocking a rail down were scored as faults. If a horse refused to jump it counted against him, too, and there was one class where timers were used and speed counted as well.

They were impressive and sparkling classes, and I rushed over to the main ring to watch them whenever I wasn't needed for Wayfarer.

Angela won an equitation class and two hunter classes with Wayfarer. Friday was the last day of junior classes; Angela and Wayfarer had a well-deserved day off Saturday, while Meg and I took a vanload of ponies and horses to another schooling show.

In between shows I'd started daily exercise and first schooling over low rails on a super chestnut colt for its nervous new owner. The horse was young but was a beautiful mover and a lovely jumper. Meg told me to go gently with him and place him at his jumps as carefully as I knew how, and it was glorious to ride such a good horse. His owner was ecstatic, and Meg was more quietly pleased.

"You've come a long way, Abby," she said. "You're like that nice colt—young, but you show a great deal of promise."

This helped take some of the sting away when the owner got over her nervousness and decided to ride her own horse almost every day. I'd been grounded again.

The stables were quiet on Monday morning a few weeks later. No clients came to ride and most of the horses and ponies rested in their stalls. Early summer had drifted over the fields and walls of the countryside; I'd been so busy I'd barely had the chance to pay much attention. I took my time in the fresh-scented morning as I rode my bike over to High Hickory. There was no hurry. I had only one thing to do, to take out a horse that needed to be hand-led for an hour. He'd hit his leg on a wall and needed quiet, controlled exercise for a few days to help the leg heal. It was pleasant not to have a lot going on this one day of the week, especially after hectic horse show weekends.

I put my bike away and went to the stable. Donna was just putting the injured horse back into his stall.

"Hey, I'm sorry," I said. "I'd have taken him out for you—that's what I came for. You've got enough to do."

"That's okay," said Donna. "It was kind of nice, just walking around in the sunshine. No problem."

I turned to go and saw Russ standing and looking into one of the stalls toward the end of the aisle.

"Say, Abby," he said, "if you haven't got anything better to do, how'd you like to take this horse out for a while."

"Sure," I said, hurrying to the stall. "What horse is it?"

"Sandpiper," Russ said. "I've ridden him some, but I'd like to watch him go with another rider on him."

Russ led Sandy from the stall. I hardly recognized him. All of us were used to seeing him grazing on the place wherever he wanted to be, but I'd been so busy I hadn't stopped to have a good look at him for some time.

It was amazing what several weeks of good feed and care had done for the horse. His sleek coat shone in the soft stable light. His mane and tail had been shortened and trimmed. He was neatly shod, and though he was still too thin, he no longer looked like a walking skeleton.

"He's never going to be a good-looking horse, but at least now he's presentable," said Russ. "It's time we found out what he can do."

I hurried to get my hunt cap from the tack room while Russ put a saddle and bridle on Sandy, and we led him outside.

Half an hour later, in the schooling ring, I pulled the brown horse to a stop and shrugged my shoulders at Russ. I struggled to find polite words to say. After all, it wasn't my horse and I didn't want to be rude. "He's different," I said cautiously. "I've lengthened my stirrups and I've shortened them—I don't know what else to try. He's got such a long stride that I slide all over the saddle."

Russ nodded. "I know what you mean. He's got a kind of swing in his stride—doesn't make him a very comfortable ride. I can't figure him out, Abby. Strange kind of horse. Let's see you try him over a few jumps here in the ring."

The jumps weren't set very high and I rode as well as I knew how, but Sandy hopped over the rails and a low gate indifferently, tossing me around on his back as though I were a cork floating in a bathtub.

I gave up trying to be dignified and started to giggle helplessly. "I think I need glue or Velcro on the seat of my jeans," I said as I rode over to Russ. "I'm still sliding all over the saddle. I can't even tell when he's going to leave the ground to take off at a jump. He makes me feel like a beginner all over again."

"Can't win them all, I guess," Russ said with a discouraged sigh. "From watching him jump in and out of the pastures the way he does, I thought maybe we had some kind of special horse on our hands. But this happens. Some horses look sensational jumping free but can't handle any kind of fence with a rider. He jumps safely enough, and I don't think he'd give you a wreck over a fence, but he sure doesn't look like much."

I got off and ran up the stirrups.

"Funny looking horse, funny way of going," Russ said disgustedly as we walked back to the stable. "I'll tell Carl to pick him up the next time he's in this part of the country with his van. We'll send this one off to a cheap sale, get our money back, and give us the stall room for a good horse."

10

"You've got a birthday coming up next week," Mom said that evening as we were finishing the dishes.

Ellie tossed her long hair over her shoulder as she reached up to put a cup on a shelf. "A new bicycle would be nice, Abby," she said. "A silver one, ten speed—maybe a red one. You could zip along with your hair blowing in the wind—"

I laughed. "Great idea, only my hair's hardly long enough to blow anywhere. Not yet, anyway. I'm trying to let it grow, but it takes forever. And I get plenty of zipping around on the horses I ride."

"But your bike is so old," Mom said. "Wouldn't you like a new one for your birthday? Really? Or a cassette deck for your stereo? That was your father's idea at breakfast this morning."

"Thanks, Mom, but my old bike's just fine for me," I said. "What I'd like most of all would be a riding coat. Navy blue. A nice one, for shows."

Mom looked at me thoughtfully as she turned off the water at the sink and reached for a towel to dry her hands. "All this riding means a lot to you, doesn't it. I can't imagine where your love of horses comes from.

Goodness knows your father and I don't know a thing in the world about them." She smiled. "Never mind. We'll see what we can do about a nice riding jacket for you. I see Angela Welles's mother at the meetings for the new library wing. She tells me you two girls go to shows together."

I laughed. "She's being polite, Mom. Angela rides. I help take care of her horse."

The summer days slipped by. With school over, I was spending whole days at High Hickory and was busier than ever. I didn't do as much grooming because Meg and Russ needed me more for exercising and helping out with the schooling of the horses and ponies.

There were big shows almost every weekend, and I went along to some of them. Meg had two clients with good horses that went in the van with Wayfarer to the big shows. When they were gone four or five days at a time, though, a new helper went with them. Her name was Joyce, and she could braid and turn a show horse out almost as well as Donna. As much as I struggled, the braids I practiced putting up on the ponies for the local shows always looked pathetic. They were knobby little knots instead of the tiny, smooth, flat braids the good horses must have for the big shows. And my braiding a tail was disaster. When I braided, the top was already starting to unravel before I got near the bottom. Thankfully I left this in Donna's and Joyce's hands and went on, much more happily, with my riding.

Things at the stable simmered down as the days grew hotter. The equitation riders won their qualifying ribbons for the important fall shows and went off on vacations. Angela went to Cape Cod and I exercised Wayfarer, keeping him carefully in the soft, sandy ring so he wouldn't hurt a leg or get a stone bruise out on the bridle paths.

Tommy and his mother rode several times a week, and Tommy took jumping lessons on Shamrock. Some mornings they went for a ride out in the woods and fields. I often rode with them. It made a nice change from working the horses in the ring.

I went out with them very early one morning when the mists were still lying like blue smoke in the fields and the woods were fresh and cool. I was riding Sandy, who was still at High Hickory. There'd been no signs of Carl and his battered gray van. Russ said he'd heard that Carl had gone to Texas to pick up some Quarter Horses and was waiting for him to get back.

In the meantime, because the school horses and ponies were getting their full amount of work and the show horses and ponies grew tired in the heat and were turned out to rest on weekdays instead of being ridden, I often found Sandy was the only horse available if I wanted to do anything different, like going out with Mrs. Richmond and Tommy. I was getting used to Sandy's funny stride and he was uncomplicated to ride. He never shied or acted up the way a lot of the other horses did out on the bridle paths. This was good for Azalea, who didn't need any extra foolishness—she thought up enough foolish things to do on her own.

Azalea was snorting and carrying on in front of us where a shallow stream crossed the path. She didn't want to go over it. Tommy and I waited, with Shamrock and Sandy standing quietly side by side.

"I don't know how you can stand it," Tommy said. "Riding so much, every single day. And horse shows. Dullsville."

"There's more to it than that," I protested. "Different horses to ride, different things to learn all the time . . ."

"I suppose." Tommy slapped at a fly on Shamrock's gray shoulder. "At least it's more fun riding out here than in that stupid ring. But I don't know. It sure doesn't beat soccer or baseball."

I didn't know what to say. Tommy was lucky to be able to walk at all, let alone ride. No matter how strong his leg became, he'd never again play baseball or soccer, or any of the other sports he liked so much. Riding was doing his leg a lot of good, but for Tommy it wasn't enough.

I rode forward. Mrs. Richmond was still having problems with her mare and had asked me to help. Azalea was acting as though there were crocodiles hidden in the shallow water of the stream. I walked Sandy through the water, Shamrock trotted along behind, and Azalea followed our lead as though there'd never been a thing to worry about.

We had a good ride and saw two deer and a cock pheasant. Even Tommy looked relaxed and cheerful by the time we got back to the stable.

There were monogrammed tack trunks in the aisle. "Hey, terrific," I said to Donna. "Where's the show? Can I go?"

"Not this trip. Sorry, Abby." Donna was going

through each trunk to make sure everything was there for each horse. "There are three horses going, and they'll be away for at least ten days. Joyce is going with them. Anyway, didn't Mrs. Richmond tell you? She'd like you to go out with her and Tommy on Friday. The hunt's bringing hounds over to the Benedict place. Isn't it wonderful?"

"What hunt, what kind of hounds?" I said, mystified.

Donna gave a cluck of disapproval. "If you'd ever get your nose out of the horse show prize lists, you'd have seen the notice up on our bulletin board. There used to be first-rate fox hunting in this area a few years ago. But Mr. Benedict put up a lot of wire fencing and he wouldn't let the hunt on his land. Now the place has been sold, and the new owner is ripping out all that ugly wire and putting in rail fencing instead. He's planning to run a bunch of Angus cattle there and he's invited the hunt to come back.

"Mrs. Richmond fox hunted all over, years ago, and she's thrilled to death to have the chance to go hunting again. It's still very early in the season and not much happens at this time of year. The hounds and the horses aren't fit yet, and they go out very low key, very informally, to get ready for the real season that starts sometime in October.

"In any event, she wants to go out with them and take Tommy on Shamrock. But she's not certain that Azalea's going to behave herself with hounds, and she wants someone competent on a quiet horse to watch Tommy if Azalea comes unglued. Which I should expect she'll do."

"But *me*?" I said. "I don't know anything about fox hunting." All I knew about it I'd seen on television and in movies, where screaming hounds and galloping horses now and then were part of the plot of a story. I was sure there was more to it than that, but I didn't know what it could be.

"Nothing to worry about," said Donna. "Believe me, nothing much happens this early in the season. You'll get to see the hounds, and that's nice. You can putter around awhile in the woods and fields, and then come home. You might have to jump a wall or two, but you can look for low spots and gates. Shamrock should do a great job with this. He's a super sensible pony. All you'll do is keep an eye on him and Tommy, and have a good time."

"Okay." I hesitated. "What do I wear?"

"Your showing stuff will be fine," she said. "This isn't formal hunting. You don't have to bother with black coats and such until the regular season opens. Just be tidy and neat."

11

It was still dark and there was soggy mist everywhere when I stumbled sleepily into the brightly lit aisle of the stable on Friday morning. There wasn't a glimmer of daylight anywhere.

The horses had been fed and groomed. I shuddered to think what time Donna must have had to get up to have them ready, but she was smiling and cheerful, as always, and wished me good morning as I wandered down the row of stalls.

I smelled fresh coffee in the tack room. I didn't like the taste all that much, but I thought a cup might help wake me up. Donna stopped me with a smile.

"I wouldn't, if I were you," she said. "That's one problem no one's been able to solve. No powder rooms out there in the hunting field."

I hadn't thought of that, of course. It seemed to me there were a lot of things I didn't know about hunting.

"How am I going to know the right things to do?" I said crossly. Donna stopped with her arms full of saddles and bridles.

"Keep your eyes open and watch the rest of the field—that's what they call the people out hunting. Stay out of the way of the hunt staff. They mean business.

Their job is to be with hounds, no matter what. But the rule to end all rules is don't interfere with hounds. Give them all the room in the world whenever you see them, even a single hound trying to catch up with the pack. Turn your horse's head toward a hound if you catch sight of it first, before the horse has the chance to kick or step on it. This is the ultimate disgrace. And that's really the basics."

I nodded numbly and hoped I wasn't going to make a fool of myself. I followed Donna to Shamrock's stall. "Come to think of it, who do I ride?" I asked suddenly.

"Meg's got you down on the list for Sandy this morning," said Donna.

I made a face. "You sure can't take any of the private show horses hunting," said Donna. "And the stable hacks are no use for this. Come on, cheer up. You said yourself he wasn't so bad."

"But he's such a peculiar jumper," I said miserably. I still had visions of tearing crowds of riders leaping enormous fences with hounds far off in the distance, as they always seemed to be, not only on television and in the movies but in the hunting prints people had hung on their walls in their tack rooms and dens too.

"You're nervous," Donna said crisply. "You'll get over it once you're on your way."

"Right," I said uncertainly. I trailed along after her and offered to help saddle Azalea. Donna waved me away, and I fumbled with Sandy's bridle and saddle and got them on him somehow just as Mrs. Richmond's car lights swept into the driveway.

Dawn was softening the edges of the sky as we

60

mounted, checked our girths, and set out along the path between the paddocks.

"It's not far to the meet this morning," Mrs. Richmond said, calling back to us over her shoulder as her mare fussed along ahead. "Isn't this nice? And to think, we'll be able to go hunting all season."

She turned her attention back to her fretting horse. Tommy rode Shamrock along in silence. He looked as sleepy as I felt.

We turned onto a road and the shoes of the horses and pony rippled like music on the pavement. The sky was streaked with rose and gold, and pale early sunlight was just starting to spill over the woods and fields as we turned through a gate into a field and moved into a trot on the softer ground.

A faint cart track led across the field, and as we followed it and topped the rise of the hill, we could see a small red van at the edge of the woods with a scattered handful of horses and riders nearby. I had expected a whole crowd of horses and riders and a great feeling of drama and excitement in the air. And where were the huge, great, foaming hounds of the hunting pictures? There wasn't so much as a puppy in sight.

Mrs. Richmond said that Tommy and I should wait where we were, and she rode forward to greet some of her friends. I jumped off Sandy, checked Shamrock's girth and took it up a hole, and got back on. Shamrock and Sandy stood quietly.

"I don't even see red coats anywhere," I whispered to Tommy.

"Even the hunt staff doesn't wear scarlet until the

formal season opens," he told me in a low voice. "That's not until next month."

There were a few faint whimpers. The back doors of the van were opened and a ripple of mottled brown-and-white hounds flowed out onto the field. Sandy and Shamrock raised their heads and pricked their ears with interest as some hounds rolled in the fresh grass or rushed over to a wide-shouldered man in a dark green coat who was holding the reins of an enormous bay horse.

"That's Bill Hennessy, the huntsman," Tommy told me in a whisper. "Mom knows a lot of these people, she's always been a nut about hunting. I don't see Mr. Windham, though. He's the hunt's Master, and we'd have to be introduced to him if he were here this morning."

One of the hounds trotted over to us. He had big, dark eyes and looked very friendly. "He doesn't look all that ferocious to me," I said to Tommy. "And look. He's even wagging his tail."

"That's not a tail," said Tommy. "Mom says the tails of hounds are called sterns. I guess every sport's got its own language. That's about all I know. Mom talks a lot about all this, but I don't always listen."

Mrs. Richmond jogged Azalea back to us. Her face was flushed with pleasure and her eyes were sparkling.

Nothing much happened. Three riders in matching dark-green coats got on their horses and vanished into the woods, taking the hounds with them. It was quiet enough to hear crows cawing from a distant field.

In spite of the silence, Azalea was foaming all over her neck and shoulders and yanking crossly at her bit.

She'd started fussing when the hounds first appeared, and kept swinging her head toward the group of horses and riders at the bottom of the hill.

"Oh, dear, I was afraid of this," Mrs. Richmond said at last. "I don't think Azalea's cut out to be a real hunter. The hounds upset her, and she always hates to stand still and wait. I'm already exhausted, and the morning's hardly begun."

I quickly offered her Sandy to ride, which I knew Meg and Russ would want me to do, but she was firm. "I don't want to spoil things for you two youngsters," she said. "Stay out for a little while and enjoy yourselves. I'll take this witless mare back to the stables. I don't think much will happen this morning, but at least you might be able to get an idea of what it's like."

She wouldn't hear of our going back with her. With a sigh, Tommy agreed to stay just to please her.

"Great," he said under his breath as Mrs. Richmond rode Azalea away from the open field. "Let's give it a few minutes so she can have a head start. Then we can split."

I yawned. My mind started to wander. I wished I were going with the show horses. I wished I were back in bed. The reins slipped lazily through my fingers. The small group of riders was moving slowly along the edge of the woods. Sandy and Shamrock broke into a comfortable slow jog as we followed well behind the others.

Tommy looked as though he was falling asleep, and so did Shamrock. I warned Tommy to shorten his reins and wake the pony up a little before he fell over his own sleepy feet.

There was a funny hush. And then a sudden rush of

sound, like caroling. Sandy flung his head in the air with his ears strained forward and Shamrock gave a small jump of excitement. The air rang with music and I saw hounds running, spilling from the edge of the woods, pouring over the wall and out across the open field to our left. There was the call of the hunting horn mixed with the glorious sound hounds were making as the huntsman came crashing out of the woods on his huge bay horse, holding his short copper horn to his lips. The horn called in short, glad notes as he sent his horse into a rolling gallop after the flying hounds.

Tommy and I snatched frantically at our reins to shorten them as we broke into a gallop. Goose bumps raced up my back and along my arms. Other riders and horses were skimming over the field behind the huntsman and hounds. Golden notes of the hunting horn floated above the bubbling music of the hounds.

We were well behind the others. Suddenly it seemed much too far behind. There was a big stone wall across the field and the hounds and the huntsman were already far on the other side. Many of the other riders had turned away, I supposed looking for a gate or a lower spot to jump.

I glanced over my shoulder at Tommy and Shamrock. The pony was striding out in an eager gallop, and Tommy's face was glowing with excitement. I knew the pony could jump the wall because I'd jumped him myself over some big fences during the summer just for fun. And I didn't want to turn away from it on Sandy. The horse might be a funny jumper, but he'd never gotten me into real trouble, and this was no time to weigh things and worry.

"Are you game for this?" I shouted to Tommy.

"You bet," he shouted back. With a grin he reached up, jammed his hunt cap more firmly on his head, and we set sail for the wall.

Sandy floated off the ground in the strange way he had while I held on to his mane. Shamrock sailed over it with a foot to spare. We landed lightly out in the far field still at a sweeping gallop, Tommy's grin wider than ever. I saw him reach down and give Shamrock a quick pat of approval.

"I think you've been kidding us," I said out loud to Sandy, feeling the wind in my face and listening to the cry of hounds somewhere ahead.

We caught sight of the huntsman's back as he swung his horse to follow a rutted lane, down a steep track, and into the woods over a low post-and-rail fence. I followed on Sandy, keeping half an eye on Shamrock behind me. There were low-hanging branches in the woods. We ducked and clung blindly to our reins, letting the horses find their own footing, and jumped out of the woods again over another wide wall.

Silence. We slowed to a walk. Where had everybody gone? We were alone at the edge of a field I'd never seen before.

"Where are we?" I whispered to Tommy.

"Just outside the Benedict place," he said in a low voice. "I've ridden out here with Mom. . . ."

There was the muffled sound of hoofbeats on the loamy path in the woods and Bill Hennessy, the huntsman, jumped over the wall and pulled up beside us.

"I took the other path," he said. "I thought hounds had gone that way. Sure was a surprise, a run like that at

this time of year. . . ." He turned his head, listening. But I already knew where hounds were. Sandy had his head up and his ears pricked toward the right. I didn't want to say anything, though. Who was I, out for the very first time, to tell the huntsman where his hounds had gone just because I thought my horse knew where they were?

Sandy was right, he knew exactly where hounds were. The huntsman's big horse turned his head a few moments later, and we all heard it then—a puzzled whimper or two and one hound calling now and then.

"That's Venture," said Mr. Hennessy with satisfaction. "She knows. Whatever clever old fox they're after, Venture knows and she's trying to tell the others."

He lifted his bright horn and blew a call that sent more goose bumps down my arms. Even Sandy was trembling, I could feel it like a low electric charge running through him. And Shamrock's eyes glowed like dark lanterns under his silvery forelock.

"Come on, kids," said the huntsman. "The pack has split and everyone else has gone with the others. We're the only ones with this group." Without another word he sent his powerful bay into a gallop in the direction we'd heard hounds.

"Okay?" I said quickly to Tommy, forcing myself to remember I was supposed to be taking care of him tenderly—fat chance, with the smile on his face that looked as though it would stay glued on forever.

"Okay," Tommy answered briefly, and we were on our way again.

12

We tackled walls and fences that would have given me waking nightmares if I'd had the chance to look them over first. But the huntsman went over on his good bay horse and we followed. Sandy took each fence we jumped to perfection in his own drifting, effortless style. Shamrock jumped them easily with his gray knees up by his chin.

Hounds were running again. We could hear the ringing of their cry. I slowed Sandy a little. Shamrock, after all, wasn't as tall as a horse, and his stride wasn't as long. I was afraid he'd tire with all the galloping and jumping we'd done. Sandy had hardly turned a hair, but Shamrock was beginning to sweat and I could see a line of foam on his neck next to the reins.

Tommy looked ready to ride until hounds ran over the edge of the world. I smiled to myself. Whatever happened, Tommy could never look back on *this* day and say it was boring.

We were back in thick woods again, which gave me an excuse to slow up even more. The path was rocky and steep. Much to my relief, Sandy slowed obediently at the touch of my reins. His manners were perfect, even with hounds running ahead.

The path forked and I pulled up to listen. I needn't have bothered, because Sandy knew which way hounds had gone. He swung to the right again and we cantered slowly through the deep shadows of the trees.

The woods brightened. Sunlight showed through the leaves. I was ducking under a low branch, thinking we must be getting close to an open field, when I heard a crash and the splinter of breaking rails. I pulled Sandy to a stop as the path made a sharp turn.

Ahead of us was the big bay horse, struggling on the ground on the near side of a dark, wide stream. On the far side of the stream was a strip of grass on a bank and then the towering rails of an enormous fence. It was freshly installed; the wood was still yellow. Several of the top rails were cracked. And on the other side of the fence, out in an open field on the grass, Bill Hennessy lay in a crumpled heap with the horn still in his hand.

The bay horse surged into the air and tumbled over again, rolling into the woods.

"Give me room," I shouted to Tommy. He understood at once and pulled Shamrock to the side of the path. I trotted back a short way, turned Sandy and steadied him, and set him at the stream and the soaring rail fence.

It looked too high to be real. It looked impossible. But if the huntsman had asked his bay horse to jump it—and he sure had to know more about it than I did—he must have considered it jumpable, and that's all I needed to know. Because it seemed to me I was on a horse that could do it.

Sandy's stride lengthened. I didn't know if we were going fast enough, but I didn't know how to tell. It seemed wisest just to let the horse alone. His ears were pricked forward, judging the fence, and I buried my hands deep in his mane. I may even have shouted "help" in midair over the fence, though I'd rather not think so. Sandy drifted over the stream and the grass and the rails and landed effortlessly in the sunlight of the open field.

I slid my hand down his dark neck in a quick gesture of gratitude as I swung him in a circle and stopped. Too much was happening and my mind was in a whirl. I jumped off and led Sandy quickly over to where Bill Hennessy was sitting up with a dazed look in his eyes.

"Are you all right?" I asked breathlessly. "You must lie still, you had a terrible fall. We'll ride to get help."

"You didn't just jump that fence," Mr. Hennessy said. "I must be out of my head."

"You had a bad fall," I said again, patiently. "Tell me how to get to the nearest road and we can get help for you."

"The new caretaker of this place is the one that's out of his head, come to think of it." Bill Hennessy got slowly to his feet. "He can't put up fencing of that height if he wants any mortal horse to get through this land."

He brushed grass from the sleeve of his coat and reset his black hunt cap more firmly on his gray hair, looking at the stream with its bank and rails and then over to Sandy, who was standing patiently at the end of the reins I was holding in my hand.

"Hey, you okay?" I heard Tommy calling from the woods. "Tell Mr. Hennessy his horse looks pretty good. He had one leg caught in the reins but they just broke, and he galloped off the way we came."

Before I could answer, hounds suddenly crashed into full cry. They didn't sound far. I pressed Sandy's reins into Mr. Hennessy's hand. "If you'll hold my horse, I'll get yours while you catch your breath."

"This is Russ's new horse, right?" said Mr. Hennessy. "The one he complains jumps out all the time and can't do anything else?"

"That's right," I said quickly. "Now let me go after your horse. . . ."

"Thank you," he said, and in one quick motion he was in Sandy's saddle and was breaking the horse into a canter. "Tell Russ I'll get his horse back to him, but right now I've got to stop hounds. They're running right toward the highway." Stirrup irons glinted against the huntsman's black boots and I stood, frozen with astonishment, watching the leggy brown horse wing away from me like a swallow over the open field, carrying his green-coated rider effortlessly over the wall at the top of the rise and out of sight.

"I don't believe it," I said out loud. "I don't believe one minute of this entire day."

And then I let out a shriek of surprise as I turned and found myself face to face with a big gray pony. "Tommy." I cleared my throat and tried again. "Tommy, tell me you didn't jump all that stuff on Shamrock."

"Sort of." If I'd thought Tommy looked happy before, now he looked triumphant. "Shamrock and I both knew we couldn't jump that whole thing the way you and Sandy did. So I just left it all up to Shamrock. He jumped the stream onto the grass, and then he jumped the rails. Like kind of an in-and-out, you know?" He patted his pony's neck. "He's a very thinking pony."

Shamrock pushed a friendly muzzle against my arm and I rubbed his forehead, under his forelock, while I struggled for something to say.

"Never mind." I pushed my cap to the back of my head and squinted up at Tommy's joyful face. "We'll talk about this later. You take this thinking pony of yours and go find yourself a gate or a gap in the fence to get back into the woods. You'll break both of your necks if you try to jump that thing in the other direction."

Tommy gave me a dignified look. "I know better than that," he said. "We'll meet you back on the bridle path as soon as we can."

I watched Shamrock's broad rump and silver tail, and Tommy's proud back, as they jogged away, along the edge of the woods, to look for a way through. I let out a tired sigh that I could feel all the way to my toes. And then I giggled. Whatever had happened to Donna's description of a quiet day with hounds so early in the season?

I crawled through the thick, splintery rails of the fence, got my good boots soaked wading through the stream, which was a lot deeper than I'd thought, and plodded up the stony bridle path.

It was a relief to see the big bay horse standing near the fork in the path. His broken reins had snagged in the branches of a bush and he was serenely nibbling the leaves on a nearby tree. He had a bump on one knee that was beginning to swell and a few small cuts on his side. I loosened his girth, ran up the stirrups, and had just finished checking him over for the second time when Tommy came trotting along the path on Shamrock.

"There was a gate in the fence just out of sight from where we were," Tommy reported. "How's Mr. Hennessy's horse?"

"Other than the bump on his knee, he seems pretty good," I said. "I'll take him on back to High Hickory, but I'm going to lead him. I don't want him to carry any extra weight."

It was a good thing Tommy knew where we were because I didn't have a clue. Riding boots, especially soaking wet ones, aren't made for walking, and I thought we'd never get home. But I had plenty of things to think about other than my soggy boots and tired legs. Most of all I thought about Sandy and his effortless, graceful way of jumping the bigger fences we'd met during the day. I wondered how I'd be able to explain all this to Meg and Russ.

13

I crept out of bed the next morning. I couldn't *believe* how stiff I was. Hot breakfast helped some but not a whole lot. Even Ellie took pity on me. She'd just gotten her driver's license, which may have had something to do with it, but she did seem sympathetic and borrowed Mom's car to drive me over to High Hickory so I wouldn't have to struggle with my bicycle.

I sure didn't want to ride one single horse that day, either. But I wanted to see if Bill had brought Sandy back safely and if the horse was all right after our wonderful day.

Tommy and Mrs. Richmond were at the stable. Tommy was telling Donna about every fence we'd jumped as she groomed Shamrock in the stable aisle. They greeted me joyfully and we went over the whole day again.

"Bill Hennessy just left," said Donna. "It was so late by the time he got hounds stopped yesterday that he took Sandy back to the hunt stables for the night. He brought him home and picked up his own horse this morning. That must have been quite a fence you jumped on Sandy, Abby. Bill said that when he looked up from the ground after his horse fell and saw Sandy in the air over those impossible rails, he thought it was the dark angel of death coming at him. Never saw such a jumper in his life. Or rode a better one either. That's what he said."

Meg and Russ joined us as we grouped around Shamrock.

"You kids sure had a run to remember," Russ said. "Bill told us. He was worried at first because of the way you two were right with him, every step of the way, and he knew neither of you had ever been out with hounds in your lives before. But he finally saw what a great time you were having and that Shamrock and Sandy could handle anything his own horse could—more, as it turned out.

"And he had a lot to say about Sandy. Abby, you've ridden the horse more than anyone else. He's never looked like much before. What's this all about?"

I forgot how stiff I was as I tried to explain the change in Sandy. Finally I sighed and shook my head. "He just wasn't the same boring horse he was when he jumped the little fences in the ring," I said. "All I know is he jumped everything well, everywhere the hunt went, and by the time we got to that huge rail fence—you know, the one where Mr. Hennessy's horse fell—I was sure he could jump it. That's all."

Tommy grinned. "*And* the stream and the bank on the takeoff side," he said.

Meg and Russ looked at each other. "Maybe we've got ourselves some kind of horse, after all," Russ said.

I dragged my aching bones down the stable aisle to see Sandy. Tommy came with me, laughing at how stiff I was, and then admitted he felt the same way. Sandy looked content, as he always did, eating his hay in a quiet corner of his stall. I gave him an apple and stroked his neck. He finished the apple and turned away to go back to his hay.

"He doesn't exactly try to climb into your pocket, does he?" said Tommy.

"I know," I said. "He's sure not what you'd call a friendly horse. It's almost as though he thinks people are a nuisance, though he's always perfectly polite."

We watched him for a few minutes in dreamy, tired silence, jumping each fence together in our minds, hearing again the sound of hounds deep in the woods and their cry in the open fields.

One afternoon a week later, the sky was thick with dark clouds and a fine rain had started to fall. Nobody was paying any attention to the weather, though, as I eased Sandy back to a canter and then to a walk.

"You see?" I said simply. Russ and Meg stared back at me in silence.

There was a groom whooping with excitement from where he'd been watching by the stable door. A cluster of riders had stopped near the gate and were murmuring to each other, and Martin, a friend of Meg and Russ who was the stable manager here at the Southwind Training Center, shoved his cap to the back of his head and kicked thoughtfully at a rail near his foot.

"That horse is a jumping freak," Martin said, breaking the funny silence at last.

I glanced back over my shoulder. The ring was huge and filled with just about every kind of horse show jump imaginable. Two more jumper courses, with banks and ditches, were spread across other fields outside the main ring. Horses and riders came to train here from all over the country. Martin had said Meg and Russ were welcome to bring their horse to try him out over the kind of jumps High Hickory didn't have. There was no other way to find out what Sandy really could do.

I slipped out of the saddle, loosened the girth, and started to walk the horse in wide circles to cool him out. I led him past some of the fences we'd jumped a few minutes before. The top rails were set higher than my head. A little over a week ago I'd have shuddered at their size. Now I smiled to myself and wondered if I'd ever see a jump again in my life, anywhere, that would look as wide and as tall as the stream and rails Sandy and I had jumped out hunting.

I whistled softly under my breath as I walked. I was content to wait for Meg and Russ to come out of their shock. Though they'd often seen Sandy jumping free over their pasture fences, they'd only seen him plop around over the little jumps in their ring with a rider on his back. Mostly me. Hardly impressive.

Tommy and I could tell them, Bill Hennessy could tell them, but they had to see it for themselves. As Sandy had soared effortlessly over any kind of jump they'd set up in the Southwind ring, all I'd had to do was let the horse alone and give him every chance to jump the way he knew best.

"Is that the horse Bill Hennessy's been talking about?" Martin asked. "The one he rode the day the pack split and the best hounds went after the old dog fox that ran them half across the county? He said the horse never laid a toe to a fence wherever they went, and they jumped everything out there except the Hutchinson's cow barn before he finally got hounds stopped just this side of the highway."

Russ nodded. He and Martin went on talking about Sandy.

Meg still hadn't said anything at all. She went to the High Hickory van and brought back a plaid cooler, which she threw over Sandy, and then covered the cooler with a rain sheet to keep it dry.

"So what are you going to do with him?" Martin asked. "I've got five clients waiting right now for their phones to ring. Each of them wants a jumper. With world-class potential. And you know what people are ready to pay today for this kind of horse."

I stopped, frozen with horror. I hadn't thought beyond this moment, when I'd be able to show Meg and Russ what Sandy could really do. I realized now, as I always should have, that Sandy could be sold quickly right out from under me. Even though I'd begun to feel since our day's hunting, that *I'd* discovered the horse's incredible brilliance, and so Meg and Russ would keep him forever at High Hickory, and part of this marvelous horse would somehow always be mine.

Sandy bumped into me and stopped. I stroked his wet neck and strained to hear what Meg or Russ would answer.

"I think," Meg said at last, "we ought to take him home and figure things out."

No one said much of anything as we unsaddled Sandy,

wrapped his legs, and loaded him into the van. We thanked Martin for letting us use his ring, and he stood waving in the rain and calling out that he hoped to hear about the horse soon.

I sank back against the seat of the van, shivering suddenly in my wet jeans and cotton shirt. Maybe I should have kept my mouth shut and not said anything about Sandy. But Bill Hennessy was hardly keeping the horse a secret, telling the world about the unbelievable brown jumping horse from High Hickory. I looked down at my muddy hands clenched in my lap.

There seemed to be no question about it. Sandy would go on to the show ring. As Martin had said to Russ that morning, over and over again, good horses were hard to find and the big money wanted jumpers. There was no way I was going to get to keep Sandy for myself.

"I think," Meg said cautiously, "that we'd better take things a bit slow right now. A horse like this is a real surprise. Let's show him a few times ourselves under the farm name. It wouldn't do High Hickory anything but good to show a first-class jumper."

I stared through the rain-streaked windows but I didn't see the wet trees going by. I saw Angela on Sandy, waiting gracefully to ride him into a horse show ring.

Russ's face was scarlet with half-suppressed excitement. "In all my years with horses, I've never seen one jump like that horse did this morning," he said. "That's what fooled us, all right. The little fences we tried him over at home weren't of any interest to him. He had to have the challenge of a demanding fence to show us what he could do. And we never asked him. Who'd have guessed? He looked like *nothing*."

He pounded the steering wheel of the van with one hand. Meg asked sweetly if he'd prefer that she drove, before he turned the van over into a ditch and demolished the horse. Russ made himself calm down and we arrived safely back at High Hickory.

Tommy was there, helping Donna groom Shamrock. "Hey, Abby," he said, with his face splitting into a wide grin. "How's about another quiet day with hounds some time soon?"

"You're on," I said, smiling back at him. His joy was contagious. Even Shamrock looked pleased with himself. Mrs. Richmond's face had been bright with happiness every time I'd seen her since Tommy'd had such a wonderful day of hunting. Suddenly there was something Tommy could do well again, a sport with new and unending challenge. I hadn't heard him mention the word "soccer" for a week.

Azalea had been sold as a show hunter and a new mare, Autumn Crocus, had come to take her place. She was a wise little thing, with a pretty head and manners to match, and she'd been hunted for a full season down in North Carolina; hounds and the sound of a horn wouldn't set her into a frazzled frenzy as they had Azalea. Now Mrs. Richmond could look forward to hunting with Tommy, though she said she'd never get over missing our wild ride our first day with hounds.

Somehow it all seemed a lifetime ago. So much had changed so quickly. I shivered again and went to get a thick jacket from the tack room.

✿　✿　✿

Meg called that night as Ellie and I were watching a western on television. I was staring without any interest at miraculously fat, unsweating horses racing mile after mile over fake rocks and deserts with fake cowboys yelling on their backs.

I took the call on the extension in the kitchen. "You must be wondering," Meg said, "about what we're going to do next with Sandy. You're pretty involved in this, after all. We thought we'd show him in the junior jumper division at the Somerset show next week. It's a big show. But there's no use wasting him on smaller stuff—not a horse that can jump the way he can. Would you like to ride him?"

I struggled to find the right words and then said the first dumb thing that was on my mind. "Not Angela?"

"No, not Angela." Meg laughed. "You're a better rider than you give yourself credit for, Abby. Angela's good, but in a different way. She looks pretty on a nice horse in equitation classes, but that's hardly enough to ride a jumper."

I closed my eyes, rejoicing with a silent smile of celebration.

"I'd like to. Very much," I said. I hoped I sounded dignified, but I wasn't at all sure. When I hung up the phone a few minutes later, the tiny click of the receiver sounded to me like a key turning, opening a golden door for me.

Mom, Ellie, and I all went together for the fitting of my new riding coat. I stared at myself in the mirror as the tailor adjusted the sleeves. I was wearing the pale blue shirt Ellie had given me to go with the new navy-blue jacket, and she'd had the neckband of the shirt monogrammed with my initials as a surprise. A new me looked back from the mirror, trim and correct in my well-fitting coat.

The tailor went to get a fresh piece of chalk. Ellie disappeared and came back with a hunt cap she'd borrowed from another department in the next room, gave me a wink and a smile of approval, and fussed with the cap and my hair.

"There," she said. "I'm glad you're finally letting your hair grow longer. I'll show you a better way to keep it smooth under your cap when we get home. I don't know anything about horses, but I see your horse show magazines and the riders are perfection. No reason you can't look the same way."

Mom watched and listened and sighed a little sadly.

"You two aren't even arguing," she said. "It seems so strange, I almost miss it. Abby, you do look nice."

14

The show grounds were in a bowl of smooth green grass surrounded by low, wooded hills. Silver birches were pencil-thin streaks of white against the dark pines. There were four big rings on the show grounds, all of them glowing with rows of red and white geraniums.

Meg was standing by Sandy's shoulder as we waited our turn in the ring. "Just remember the course and the way we walked it before the class," she said. "Watch out for the marker flags on the far turn, and make sure you get Sandy set straight for the wall."

"Yes, Meg," I said mechanically. I was watching the horse jumping in the ring. He was a sturdy little chestnut, with a sprinkling of white over his rump, and his rider was good. She spun him through the flags in a crisp turn that put the horse just the right number of strides from the wall. There was applause, the horse left the ring, and the gate in front of me swung open.

I heard the announcer's voice over the loudspeaker but couldn't understand what he said. Sandy walked into the ring with his long, reaching stride and swung into a soft canter at the touch of my heel.

The sounds of the show and the busy, chattering

stands full of spectators faded into misty silence around me as I closed my mind to them. There was nothing in the world just then but Sandy and me and the course of fences to be jumped.

The jumps were banked with riots of flowers, the rails were clean and high, and Sandy floated his way around the course. I remembered the flags at the turn and guided Sandy through, but I knew better than to tell him what to do with my hands or my legs as we reached the wall.

He drifted over it from the takeoff he chose, and I could have hugged him as we left the ring. But I pretended to be calm and reasonably cool as I got off and led him over to Meg and Joyce, who had come along to care for Sandy.

"Good trip," Meg said crisply as Joyce threw the cooler over Sandy's back.

"Felt right," I said, just as crisply, though I felt as though every bone in my body was shaking apart with excitement.

The boxy little chestnut, whose name turned out to be Frosty Pumpkin, had scored half a fault, and he was second in the class. It was Sandy who marched calmly into the ring with me to accept the blue ribbon along with a prize-money check.

"Nice," said Meg as she and I stood to watch Joyce lead the horse quietly away.

"Yes, it was," I said. "Nice." I looked right at Meg's serene, almost expressionless face, and she winked at me. I knew she felt just the way I did, wanting to whoop

and holler like the cowboys in the silly television westerns. But this was not the moment.

Other trainers and owners came to congratulate Meg and were introduced courteously to me. Questions were asked about Sandy. The girl who'd ridden the chestnut horse smiled and waved as she went past.

As soon as I could, I slipped away. I needed to be alone for a while. One show. One class. But how perfectly, unbelievably wonderful it was.

Our second class was just after the lunch break. The sun was high and the red and white flags marking the turns of the course hung limply in the still air.

Meg and I walked the course with the other riders and trainers as soon as the ring crew had it set up. "This triple is a tough one," Meg pointed out to me as we paced off the distances between the jumps. "One stride when you land over the first part, and two before you jump the third. Okay?"

"Sure, Meg," I said reassuringly. But I wanted to laugh. Sandy would decide how he wanted to time his strides at his fences, not me. Only Bill Hennessy and I knew what it was like to ride this fantastic horse. I knew he'd not been able to put it into words. Neither could I.

I wasn't trying to pretend to be something I wasn't. Meg knew I had no experience in the world of the big shows. But I was smart enough to let the horse alone when he jumped and to ride as well as I knew how, and it had to be enough for now.

Sandy touched the tip of one hoof on the top of a glittering white rail. I didn't even hear it, but Meg said it had been on the gate with the rails, and so Sandy had one fault in the class and was second to Frosty Pumpkin this time.

It had still been a good class and the horse had gone well. The red ribbon for second place danced on Sandy's bridle as I led him from the ring behind the chestnut.

I patted Sandy before Joyce led him away, talked briefly to Meg, and went to get a Coke. The girl who rode Frosty Pumpkin was at the refreshment tent and came over to me. We introduced ourselves to each other and said nice things about each other's horses. Her name was Julie Dixon and she rode in horse shows most of the year, she told me, starting in Florida in January and finishing the season at Toronto in November. She and three other friends shared a tutor who traveled with them. Her father owned several good hunters and jumpers, and they were hoping to win the annual High Score Award for Junior Jumpers with Frosty Pumpkin at the end of the year. "But not if you keep chasing me with that brown horse of yours," she said with a smile. "He's enough to make any of us nervous."

Our classes were done for the day. We wandered around the show grounds and watched a class of small pony hunters in a far ring while thunderclouds piled up in the sky and finally sent us running for shelter.

"See you tomorrow, Abby," Julie said as she ran to her father's car.

I found Meg in Sandy's stall at the stabling tent, rubbing the horse's head soothingly as the thunder began roaring overhead. "Nothing in the world seems to bother this horse," she said, ducking at a savage bolt of lightning. Sandy went back to eating his hay.

"There, you see?" Meg said wonderingly. "I'm not sure this horse is for real."

"He eats enough for a real horse," Joyce said as she came into the stall with a heaping measure of grain. "Horse shows sure don't put him off his feed at all."

"He's still catching up on all the weight he needed," said Meg. "He looks better all the time. It's amazing what a change good feed and good care can make. Every day he looks more and more the way he should. He looks like a completely different horse."

Sandy buried his muzzle in the feed tub and we left him to eat in peace.

We were miles and miles away from home. Joyce was staying at the show grounds, sleeping on a cot in a curtained tack stall beside Sandy's. I thought this looked like fun, but Meg insisted I stay at the motel where she'd reserved rooms for us. I was glad when we got there and I could collapse on a big, soft bed. She and I had an early dinner at the motel restaurant, and Meg went to join a group of horse show friends while I took a long, hot bath and fell onto the bed again. I hadn't realized how tired I was, and I pulled up the blankets and fell asleep just after I'd turned off the light.

15

The next day was sparkling after the thunderstorm; a bright breeze was blowing, and the show grounds were festive with banners and flags dancing in the cool air. And by the end of the spectacular afternoon there was a blue, red and yellow championship ribbon fluttering with Sandy's other ribbons on the tack-room wall.

I helped take the tiny braids from Sandy's mane, humming under my breath to the John Denver songs on the portable radio propped against a hay bale nearby. Joyce was sorting through the tack trunk, straightening things out, when Meg came hurrying over to us.

"I've just been to the committee tent," Meg said breathlessly. "They paged me on the loudspeakers. They're holding a special class here tomorrow afternoon. They're calling it the Crystal Challenge Cup. I saw something in the prize list about it, but I didn't pay all that much attention because only horses that had won Junior Jumper Championships were eligible. And Sandy hadn't, not back then."

I patted Sandy and got down from the overturned milk-bottle carrier I'd been standing on to reach the top part of his mane. Meg pulled it away to a safe spot in the tack room—she had a horror of a horse getting a hoof caught in these boxes, which I should have remembered—and I waited in suspense for her to go on.

"It really is a crystal cup," Meg said. "It's beautiful. I saw it in the committee tent. Some corporation or other has put up a bundle of money for the class and they're hoping it will turn out to be a big class for this show every year. And they wanted to know if we'd like to enter Sandy."

"Fantastic." I glowed with excitement.

"That's one vote yes. How about you, Joyce? Everything okay for one more day?"

"Fine with me," said Joyce. "And I brought enough feed and such for a week. I always bring too much, I guess, but sometimes it turns out to be a good idea."

I called home, and Mom and Dad said it was all right to stay. We were even lucky enough to keep our rooms at the motel. Dinner that night turned into a celebration. A lot of show people were staying there, and we all came trooping into the dining room pretty much at the same time. The waitresses pushed a whole row of tables together and I ended up sitting between Julie and a tall boy with blond hair whom I'd seen riding for the past two days of the show. His name was Conrad Fletcher.

He had a powerful blue-gray horse called Sea Glass that he was showing in Junior Jumpers. Julie told me later that he had one eye on future Olympics. Conrad had spent the first part of the summer working the horse with its trainer in Europe. I knew he'd won ribbons during the show and complimented him on his beautiful horse.

We all had a good time, but Meg packed me off to bed by ten o'clock. I went off protesting that she made me feel like a baby in kindergarten, but again I discovered I was more tired than I knew. I took another long bath, washed my hair, and tried to freshen up my new blue riding coat with a damp washcloth. I ended up going to bed and falling asleep before my hair was dry.

The next morning was hot, and a blue haze covered the hills around the show grounds. Meg and I walked the jumper course with the other coaches and riders. "Tricky, tricky," Meg said, muttering under her breath. "You're going to have to be quick, Abby, and think your way through this every second. You haven't had much experience with this kind of course, but don't worry about it. Just do your best."

I didn't want to tell her so, because all the other riders looked grim and concerned, but I wasn't the least bit worried. I figured if I made a dumb mistake, Sandy'd get me out of it, as he always had. I walked the course with Meg a third time, getting it memorized—order of jumps, where the turns were marked, and where the timers were set up for the start and the end of the course. Meg discussed distances between fences and where to put in short and long strides to get the horse to take off from the best possible spot. I nodded wisely and knew I'd leave it all up to Sandy. He was the expert, not me.

When we had finished, I walked off by myself, shut my eyes, and went through the course in my mind several times in a row. I checked it out with the diagram at the gate, found I had it right, and went over it once more just to be sure. Turns came up very quickly, I'd discovered, and jumps seemed to appear out of nowhere, when all of it was seen from the back of a galloping horse. I could safely leave the jumping part to Sandy, but I'd better be right about the course.

There was an extra feeling of excitement in the air when the first stable calls came to get ready for the Challenge Cup. Even though I knew I had plenty of time, I found my steps quickening as I went to the stabling tent.

There was even a band playing music in a stand next to the ring. I shivered happily. It was incredibly wonderful to be part of it all.

The competitors for the Challenge Cup were asked to parade their horses in the ring before the class started. Some horses fussed and sweated, especially when they were near the bandstand, but Sandy cantered along serenely. As Meg had said, nothing seemed to bother him.

Numbers were drawn for the order of jumping. I was to go fifth. I popped Sandy over a few low schooling fences to loosen his muscles, walked to the ring, and stood ready to go as the horse before me finished his round.

Meg was standing with one hand resting on Sandy's shoulder. Joyce stood ready to pull the cooler from his back as he went into the ring.

The jumping horse finished his round with two rails down and a refusal. Not much of a threat. I started to shorten my reins as the ring gate swung open.

Sandy flung himself over backwards so suddenly that none of us had any warning. Meg and Joyce were knocked down and I was sent spinning to one side as he fell. Sandy got quietly to his feet and stood without moving, the reins dangling from his bridle.

Meg was tangled in a folding chair, and I lay on the ground stunned with surprise. Joyce jumped up to grab the horse's reins.

The ringmaster beckoned impatiently to another horse. Meg sorted herself out of the folding chair and hurried over to me. "Abby, are you all right?" she asked with concern.

"I'm fine. I think." I got shakily to my feet. All my bones seemed to be intact. "Meg, what happened?"

"I don't know." Meg and I hurried over to Sandy, who didn't appear to be hurt or in any distress. Joyce had already taken the saddle off and was going over every inch of the fleecy saddle pad to see if anything sharp or hard had accidently been caught in it. The saddle itself was a wreck. It was on the ground, twisted at an angle, and a seam of the leather had split from the force of the horse's weight as he fell over on it.

I ran to the warm-up ring on wobbling knees. Julie was there with Pumpkin, and I asked her breathlessly if she had a spare saddle I could borrow.

"Sure thing," she said. "With the bunch of horses we show, we have several extras. There's a Hermes that should be the right size for you, but take any of them you want."

By the time I'd found the saddle and brought it back, Meg had already gotten a fresh sheepskin saddle pad from our own tack trunk. We saddled the horse again with care, making absolutely sure nothing was pinching him anywhere. We checked the girth three or four times to make sure it was smooth.

I got back on and fiddled endlessly with the length of my stirrups, trying to get them right in the strange saddle. "Something must have frightened him," Joyce said comfortably, rubbing the horse's muzzle softly. Meg arranged a later time for our jumping order and watched Sandy with narrowed eyes as I trotted and cantered him both ways in the warm-up ring.

"Darned if I can see a thing wrong," she said finally. "He's sound as a bell of brass. I even checked his mouth to make sure he didn't have a jagged tooth or a cut on his tongue that might have hurt when you shortened your reins. But I couldn't find a thing. If he does anything like that again, we'll have the show vet look at him."

We stayed well away from the ring gate this time and didn't move forward until it opened and my number was called over the loudspeaker. We were all a little tense until I was actually in the ring, but once the gate closed behind us, my mind closed everything else out, too.

Sandy swung forward into a canter, and I started over the course. The jumps were high and wide, and he soared over them in his easy, floating way. I remembered the course and let Sandy do the rest, and we trotted from the ring to the sound of enthusiastic applause with a faultless round.

After the first rounds were over, the announcer declared that three horses were tied with no faults—Sandy, Frosty Pumpkin, and Sea Glass. All three of us were to jump again over a shortened course, with the fences raised, and if two or more of our horses had faultless rounds, time would be the deciding factor.

"Did he feel okay to you?" Meg asked anxiously.

"Absolutely super."

"He sure didn't jump as though anything was bothering him," Meg said with a puzzled shake of her head. "Just one of those things, I guess."

My mind was on the coming round. I wasn't too concerned about Sandy's jumping faults. He didn't like to make mistakes at his fences. My problem was going to be picking up shortcuts to save time wherever I could.

I watched Julie ride Pumpkin. She whirled her compact little horse through the course like a spinning coin. Her time was excellent, but Pumpkin pulled a rail down over the very last fence.

Conrad on Sea Glass was next to go. He jogged solemnly into the ring and set his horse into a precise slow gallop. Sea Glass had a long, reaching stride that covered a lot of ground, as he did in the air over his fences. But I wondered if this particular horse could be gathered and turned quickly enough to shorten his time around the course.

Conrad didn't seem to try to make up time with quick turns. He was content to let his horse go in a flowing, deliberate manner and finished carefully with no faults.

"Go for broke," I said to Sandy, and we cantered into the ring.

I had him in a flying gallop as we broke the electronic beam at the beginning of the course to start the clock. We swooped over the first two jumps. I sat up straight in the saddle, and he came right back to me and swung in a sharp turn. Down to the next jump, a tremendous triple rail of red-and-white striped bars. Another sharp turn and a two-strided in-and-out was next in the center of the ring. The horses were to jump the first set of rails, put in two strides, and jump the next fence. Frosty Pumpkin had done it this way. So had Sea Glass, and so had Sandy the first time around. But things were different now.

I let Sandy go into his peculiar, floating gallop. His dark ears were pricked toward the jumps and he drifted effortlessly over the first set of rails. With my hands and my legs I asked him for everything he had, and he understood. One long stride and we were in the air again over the second part of the in-and-out.

The rest, as they say, was gravy. We'd picked up treasured time and finished the course a full two seconds faster than Sea Glass. Sandy had won the Challenge Cup.

The band played as I rode back first into the ring. A woman in a flowing dress was there beaming at me, carrying a tall, lacy crystal cup that I thought was the most alarming sight I'd ever seen until I realized she had no intentions of entrusting it to a mere rider on a horse. Even my gloves were slippery with sweat, both mine and Sandy's, and I knew for sure I'd drop it if she handed it to me. A special blue ribbon with three streamers was fastened to Sandy's bridle. Sea Glass was second, and Pumpkin was third—I didn't recognize the others who won the rest of the ribbons.

The ringmaster smiled and touched his hat to me, then gestured for me to lead a victory gallop of the ribbon winners once around the ring. Almost numb with delight, I touched Sandy with my heels.

The ribbons' streamers rustled like birds' wings. I could hear them even with the glittering music of the band. I rested one hand on the back of Sandy's arched neck and we spun into a triumphant gallop.

16

School started. I bumbled around the halls in a haze. It was a good thing the first weeks were mostly review of last year's work.

"Wonderful," I told Sandy one afternoon. "You are one incredible horse." I was leading him up and down the pasture lane after our second show, where we'd won more classes. It didn't seem possible to have had so much happen so quickly, but there were newspaper clippings on the door of our refrigerator at home and in the stable office, and photographs of me on Sandy. One of them was in color, taken in midair over the last fence as we won the Challenge Cup. I'd heard that a horse magazine was going to run this picture on their next cover.

I knew Meg and Russ had some huge offers to buy the horse and were discussing them all, but I didn't ask any questions. The only way I could handle any of this was to keep my mind on my riding, one jumping class at a time.

Sandy was hand-walked the day after we got home; on the other days between shows I rode him quietly in the fields and out in the woods. His legs stayed cool and clean and Donna watched over him with her usual care.

The horse looked better than ever, although nothing would ever change the fact that his neck and back were a little short and his legs were too long. "Handsome is as handsome does," Donna said with more than a little coolness when a visitor commented on Sandy's conformation.

Meg and Russ agreed that the way the horse was put together probably helped a lot when we had to ride against the clock. He whipped around turns that might well have caused problems because of his extremely long stride. He was able to gather himself together and then float forward again into a gallop without hesitation. This was something, I was happy to note, Sea Glass and Conrad hadn't yet managed to learn.

"He's almost like a cat on his feet," Meg marveled after we'd won still another spectacular class at a show the next week. We both were shivering a little, half with cold and half with excitement. The jumper ring was gay with gold and red chrysanthemums and the trees at the edge of the field were bright with autumn colors.

There was a band again and it started to play. The stands were crowded with spectators. The announcer called us into the ring for our ribbons.

A man escorted a tall lady in a floppy hat out to present the winning trophy. She stood beaming uncertainly with one hand holding a vast silver bowl and the other clutching the brim of her hat, which was threatening to blow off at any moment in the brisk wind.

Everyone was relaxed and happy—it had been an exciting class, both to ride in and to watch. The announcer called my name and Sandy's, and I pressed him with my heels to ride forward for the presentation.

Sandy took one step forward, ducked his shoulder, spun around, and flung himself into the air. I never knew why I didn't go off. Sheer luck had to have something to do with it, because I was totally helpless, half draped over his shoulder, when his forehoofs hit the ground again. I had just managed to get my weight back in the saddle when he lunged forward and reared again with the same fluid motion he used when he jumped.

He reared so high that he swayed. I thought he was going over backwards again. I was afraid that if I moved and tried to jump off, he'd lose his balance and fall on me. I clung desperately to Sandy's braids and I think I even closed my eyes in terror.

He whirled and lunged again. I couldn't stop him—I couldn't even breathe. Someone must have told the band to stop playing. There was a terrible silence all around me. All I could hear were Sandy's harsh breaths and the muffled sound of his hoofs on the short grass.

There was no way of knowing how long it lasted. I saw Meg run into the ring, but she couldn't reach the horse's bridle. He was spinning and rearing too quickly for her to get near.

It was over as suddenly as it had started. I flung myself out of the saddle at the very first chance I had. Meg grabbed hold of the horse's reins, though by then he was standing perfectly quietly. Dimly, as though from a far distance, I could hear Meg's calm voice talking to the ringmaster. It had been the band music, of course, they agreed politely. It must have startled the horse. Yes, hadn't he done well. It had been a splendid class.

The two people presenting the trophy had wisely left

100

the ring, and, dizzy as I was, I saw the other ribbon winners scrunched together a good distance away.

"Meg," I said between clenched teeth, "I've got to get out of here. I'm going to be sick."

Fortunately, the show-ring crew had started into the ring with their tractors to take down the jumps. A victory gallop now was out of the question. I managed to squeeze out a smile for the ringmaster and hurried out of the ring beside Meg, who was leading Sandy.

I went into the ladies' room and spent the next fifteen minutes with the dry heaves.

I splashed cold water on my face and came out feeling a little better. Meg was waiting for me with a questioning look.

"I'm okay," I said. "But I don't understand. I don't think I've ever been so scared in my entire life. I couldn't stop him, there wasn't one thing I could do. Whatever got into the horse?"

"I think," Meg said grimly, "that he was telling us the party's over."

And that's exactly what it was. Over. We had another class scheduled in the afternoon, but Sandy never went through the ring gate. He spun once near the ring, ducked his shoulder, and sent me shooting off so hard and fast that I went right through the ends of the reins before I even hit the ground.

I got unsteadily to my feet, struggling for breath, and put a hand on Sandy's reins. I looked at Meg. She was staring at the horse with her face a chalky white. I wondered what mine looked like, although I didn't care. I knew there was mud on it because it was making my cheek itch as it dried.

I also wondered vaguely what I would say if Meg told me to try to get Sandy back into the ring, because I simply wasn't going to do it. I had felt moments of fear before, but never this paralyzing feeling that I didn't have the courage to try again.

I had fallen off before. I'd been bucked off horses, and I'd even had a horse I was schooling fall flat over a jump, which was not a whole lot of fun, either. But I'd never been so savagely afraid as I was now of Sandy. I couldn't even begin to understand it. With every muscle in his body, every effort of his every move, the horse was telling me that he had won the victory, he wasn't about to go back into the ring again, and I'd better believe this was the way it was going to be.

Meg didn't say anything. I led Sandy back to his stall. Nobody said much of anything as we loaded the van and drove back to High Hickory.

I made myself ride Sandy again a few days later. I let him choose his own way and we had a pleasant, quiet ride on the bridle paths in the woods. But just as we were coming back to the stable, Russ asked me to give Sandy a spin around the High Hickory jumps.

What a joke. I did dare to hope wildly, for just a moment, that everything was going to be all right again. There'd been no reason for the horse to give me such a scare. I'd just been overtired and tense.

Sandy took one look at the schooling-ring gate, gathered himself in a knot, and whirled. I yelled, Russ shouted, Meg and Donna came running, but nothing made any difference. Sandy fought like a wildcat and ended up high on his hind legs, swaying, just as he'd done at the show.

Sweat was pouring into my eyes. I clung to the horse's mane. Somehow he kept his balance and dropped to the ground again.

"Get off that crazy horse. That's enough," Russ said. His voice sounded star years away through the ringing in my ears. I nodded dumbly and slid out of the saddle, glad to feel solid ground under my feet again.

There was no more talk of my riding Sandy in any more horse shows, which was fine with me. If anybody else wanted to show him, they were welcome to it. I went to High Hickory as I always had, but mostly I rode quiet horses out on the bridle paths. I was ashamed of myself, and angry, but it didn't change anything. The very sight of the jumps in the schooling ring made me feel sick to my stomach, no matter what horse I was riding.

Sandy was usually turned out, and I'd see him in the pastures, shining and fit, grazing serenely in the autumn sunshine. Tommy often came riding with me. He rode almost every day, as he had ever since our first day of hunting. We talked of hounds and hunting, and how well Shamrock was going. Often we just rode quietly, not talking much. Either way, he was good company.

Meg came to the house one evening. Mom and Dad were just leaving for a PTA meeting at the school. Ellie faded out of the living room courteously, murmuring something about washing her hair, and Meg and I were left by ourselves to talk.

"Are you sulking, scared, or mad?" Meg sat down and came right to the point, as she always did.

I thought for a few moments. "Partly all three, I guess," I said. "Mostly I'm trying to figure out what went so wrong."

Meg sighed. "The horse went wrong. And you can bet your socks this isn't the first time for him. It's easy and cheap to starve this kind of horse into submission to get rid of him. After all, even good horses can go through hard times, so there's no way of knowing what you've got until any thin horse is fed right and given several months to recover.

"Carl's picked up a few nice horses this way, some of them from pretty tacky stables. But we've never run into a horse that could jump like Sandy; not many people do in a lifetime."

She got up and walked restlessly around the room. "I should have guessed we were in real trouble with the horse when he went over backwards with you that first time without any warning. But I made up all kinds of excuses—Sandy was such an exceptional, extraordinary jumper. And then when he behaved himself during the next classes at the show, I let myself forget about it.

"I shouldn't have. I was responsible for you. And a horse that rears as viciously as Sandy does is desperately dangerous. We're all of us lucky you didn't get hurt."

"So what happens now?" I said.

"With Sandy? I don't know yet. Yesterday Russ vanned him over to the training stables to take him around one of their courses, but I don't think things went too well. He hasn't talked about it much. He had himself half convinced the horse was spoiled, that he must have taken advantage of you because you don't weigh much and haven't had much experience. I guess he found out the horse was done with horse show jumping no matter who was on his back."

"Sandy can be pretty convincing," I said with a shiver.

Meg came back to sit down. "I tried to tell him," she said soberly, "but he didn't want to hear it."

We sat in silence a few moments, remembering.

"Anyway," Meg said more cheerfully. "I came mostly to tell you that Mr. Dixon called me this evening. He didn't know how to get hold of you. Julie had a fall a few days ago—one of their show hunters slipped on a turn and went down with her. Nothing serious, but she's got a couple of cracked ribs and they wanted to know if you'd ride Pumpkin for them in the big show weekend after next. Angela's back from the Cape, and we'll be going with Wayfarer. You could go along with us if you like. I brought the Dixon's phone number so you can talk to them yourself."

"Really?" I felt a quick surge of excitement. "What do you think? Could I do a good job with their horse?"

"Why not?" said Meg. "This is the way it starts, if you want to go on in show jumping. There's a bunch of international riders who never had good horses of their own. They were catch riders, like you, waiting for the chance to catch a good ride on a promising horse. Sometimes all the way to the top. Sandy got you out there into the big time. His part's over. Now the rest of it's up to you."

It was late when Meg left. Late enough, anyway, for me to let myself decide not to call the Dixons until the next day. I tucked the phone number into the pocket of my jeans and went upstairs to my room.

Funny. I wasn't sure how I felt about showing any horse, even Frosty Pumpkin. I thought of flags and banners in the sunlight, and clean, high fences in a horse show ring. It had been nice when Sandy had won, but not the end of the world when he didn't. It had been all of it—the skill and the challenge, worlds to conquer, little victories. A turn just right, a tough fence met on a lengthening stride, all on a horse I believed in.

But more than anything else, even more than fear, I felt betrayed.

My blue riding jacket had come back from the cleaners. It hung on my closet door in its shimmery plastic bag. The grass stains and mud were gone and it looked fresh and trim again.

This reminded me guiltily about my good riding gloves, which I'd rolled into a ball and thrown under the bed. I found them and smoothed the thin dark leather over my knee.

I sat and looked out the dark window at the starlight for a long time before I went to bed.

17

The next afternoon was golden, soft, and full of the sweet smells of Indian summer. I hated being indoors on such a day and hurried over to High Hickory as soon as I could after school. But the stables were quieter than I'd ever known them to be. Even Donna had lost her cheerful smile.

"Whatever's the matter?" I asked anxiously. "Where is everybody?"

"The lessons were canceled for today," Donna said. "Meg's at the hospital. With Russ. He may be badly hurt."

"Sandy," I said with a hollow, certain feeling.

Donna sighed. "Crazy horse. They couldn't do a thing with him when Russ took him over to the training center, which I'm sure you guessed. The horse was the rainbow with the pot of gold to Russ, and it was more than he could bear.

"He took the horse out at dawn this morning, before I even got here to feed. He left a note in the tack room that he'd be back when he had the horse conquered. That's the word he used. When I got here Sandy was standing right outside his stall, with the saddle all busted up, waiting to get in."

She ran her fingers absently over the bristles of the brush in her hand. "I called Meg and we went out to look for Russ. He hadn't gotten very far, just inside the gate of the schooling ring. The place was torn up like a battlefield. Anyway, we sent for the ambulance. Meg called from the hospital after they'd taken Russ for X rays and told me to cancel her classes. And to make a couple of calls for her." Donna looked away. "She wanted some arrangements to be made. One or two things."

It wasn't like Donna to be so indirect. I wanted to ask her right out what it was she didn't want me to know. I had the feeling she was hiding something from me, something about Sandy, but I didn't know how to ask.

There was a short, uncomfortable silence. Donna turned to put the brush back on the shelf. "Meg said she'd call again when she had more news about Russ. But there hasn't been any word yet."

I wanted to stay at High Hickory. I called Mom to explain that there'd been an accident, though I didn't go into detail, and said I might be a little late getting home.

Donna and I worked in the stables for a while in worried silence. I looked into Sandy's stall, but it was empty except for Forever, who'd had her new kittens under Sandy's feed tub. He'd been very careful to eat around them when he searched through his hay for any last scrap of grain.

Donna told me the horse was turned out in the back pasture. I felt almost guilty about my concern for him. He could well have killed me, and he'd certainly hurt Russ pretty badly. Yet I wondered if I'd ever be able to shrug him off as "just another horse." I hoped so.

109

Donna made tea in the tack room. "You know," she said at last, "my dad had a horse a lot like Sandy once. Only Dad was a racehorse trainer, and his was a promising chestnut colt that had won some pretty fancy races as a two-year-old. Talk about rainbows—Dad got rainbows *and* stars in his eyes whenever he looked at that colt.

"He had his string of horses in Florida in the spring of the colt's three-year-old season. Dad ran him in a short prep race against a quality bunch of other good youngsters. There'd been a lot of talk of sending the colt to the Derby and all of us just about had our suitcases packed. The horse came around the last turn in the race, just coasting in front of the others by six lengths. And then he stopped and spun around, jumped the rail, and galloped himself right into the pond in the middle of the infield. Jockey and all.

"You never did see such a fuss in your life. Racetrack stewards, trainers—Dad too, of course—the jockey still on the colt's back, madder than you can believe. It took them forty-five minutes to get the horse out of the water."

Donna laughed. "It seems terribly funny now, but you never saw so many angry people in one spot. There were swans and some fancy geese cruising around on the water, and they flapped their wings and honked and hissed and carried on—they didn't help much. The owner of the colt was fit to be tied. Nobody likes to be made to look foolish, and this horse really knew how. He made fools out of everybody that day.

"The owner insisted Dad get rid of the horse and the

110

colt went from one trainer to another, because every new trainer was sure *he* knew how to get the horse running again. But the colt got so tough to handle he got too dangerous to ride. He'd made up his mind he'd had enough of horse racing and that was that. He never set foot on a track again."

"What happened to him?" I asked uneasily.

"Dad bought him for fifty bucks a year later. Half as a joke and half, he said, to remind himself that you never can be sure what a horse is going to do next. We had our own place by then, and the horse was turned out with a bunch of broodmares. We kids used to ride him around the farm and never had a problem. It was only if he was asked to go out on a racetrack that he went totally bananas."

The phone rang and Donna snatched it off the hook. "Good news, that's wonderful," she said. She filled me in on details after she'd hung up. "Russ is out of the operating room. He's got a cracked pelvis and a broken leg, which is bad enough, for sure, but no damage done to his back. He's going to be okay. He's awake, and he talked to Meg a little. It's just as we thought. The horse did throw himself over backwards on top of Russ. And Russ told Meg the horse did it deliberately."

"You bet," I said with a shiver.

"But it's such an insane thing for a horse to do," Donna said. "A horse's sense of self-preservation is so strong. He's got to be aware of the danger of breaking his own neck or back by doing such a stupid thing. But I guess, like Dad's chestnut colt, there are a few willing to take awful risks to make sure they get their point across.

Which they most certainly do." She sighed. "I don't know if that makes them dumber or smarter than the rest."

She looked up at the stable clock. "I still have time to go pick up the Chapman horse this afternoon, if you could get the rest of the horses and ponies in."

"Sure," I said. "No trouble. You go ahead."

She drove off with the trailer and I brought the horses and ponies in from the paddocks, put them away, and went outside again swinging a lead shank in my hands. The late afternoon was still. Ivy streaked scarlet patterns across the sunny stone walls. There were silvery-blue streaks of mist across the fields, and I could see corn shocks in rows curving their shadows over the far hills beyond the woods.

Sandy was the only horse still left to bring in. I took a crumbling sugar cube from my back pocket and went out to get him. He turned his lean head with its narrow blaze toward me as I ducked through the rails and went over to him. He waited, watching me, and took the sugar gently from my hand. I clipped the lead shank to his halter.

I led him to the pasture gate and hesitated. Fear was a funny thing. I couldn't make sense of it all. Standing there, with the quiet horse in the silent afternoon, it was just about impossible to imagine he was the same horse that had terrified me so in the ring and sent Russ to the hospital that very morning.

I climbed onto the fence. I had the funny metallic taste of fear in my mouth and my lips were dry. Sandy didn't make sense, nothing he'd done made sense. I was bewildered, tired of worrying, tired of wondering, and

112

heartsick over this incredible horse who'd given me so much—and then brought everything to such a crashing stop.

Sandy was still standing patiently by the fence. I threw myself onto his bare back. He cantered across the russet grass of the field and jumped gently into the adjoining pasture. I hadn't realized I'd been holding my breath until I let it out with a gasp. My hands were sweaty on the leather lead shank and I wiped them one at a time on my jeans. We'd jumped a fence and we'd both survived. It was so good to feel the flow of Sandy's stride again, and the power and sureness of his jumping. He slowed and settled back into his long-strided, swinging walk.

I saw the bulldozer then, out in the far corner of the field. It was late in the afternoon and there was no one with it. The operator must have gone home, leaving his job unfinished until early the next morning. There was a huge hole dug beside it.

I stared at the hole, ugly with shadows lying dark inside it, and I knew what it was for. And I knew, then, what "arrangements" Meg had told Donna to make when she'd first called from the hospital that morning.

Sandy was motionless under me. His head was raised, his ears pricked forward, and I felt him trembling, just the littlest bit, as if a low electric current were going through him.

I tore my eyes away from the bulldozer and listened. I heard them then, too. The sound of hounds and the low, sweet-sad notes of the hunting horn calling lost hounds home.

"They must be back in the old Benedict place," I said

out loud to Sandy. My voice wavered a little, and suddenly I was crying in terrible, wracking sobs that shook me all over. "Don't you see what they're going to do to you?" I shouted to Sandy. "You won't have any of this any more. They're going to bury you in that stinking hole tomorrow, and its your own fault, your own stupid fault."

I sent the horse into a wild gallop across the pasture grass.

I still was crying so hard that I could barely see. Tears soaked into the neck of my sweater. Everything was blurry and I clung to Sandy's mane, not caring. The wall at the end of the field was high and wide, and he floated over it like a feather.

We were into the woods where blazing red and gold burned in the autumn trees. Branches tore at my cap and sweater. I ducked my head and shoulders and let the lead shank lie slack on Sandy's neck. It was no use trying to guide him. He'd have to find his own way.

There were scented shadows of deep pines and open sunlit fields again, the shorn stubble of cut corn and a tilted rail fence held up mostly by tangled crimson and yellow bittersweet vines. Nothing stopped Sandy. He never turned his head away from a jump. I knew in my heart that he never would, no matter how tall or wide or deep in the shadows the big walls and fences stood. Not out here. Not as long as there was the sound of hounds and the horn ahead.

We jumped out of the woods into another open field and Sandy stopped. Hounds were clustered in a happy

114

pattern of color around the legs of Bill Hennessy's big bay horse. Mr. Hennessy was wearing a scarlet coat—I remembered fuzzily that Tommy had told me the formal season had begun a week or so ago.

Sandy stood watching hounds. I pushed a strand of hair out of my eyes and shoved it back under my cap. Three hounds trotted over to the horse and he lowered his head to greet them.

I wiped my torn sleeve across my face and Bill Hennessy came a little bit more into focus. "Abby," I heard him say. "Get down off that horse. You're going to get yourself killed."

"I'm not," I said. Though the thought had flickered through my mind that it wouldn't have mattered a whole lot if Sandy had turned over at a wall and given us both the fall I was half hoping for. It would have solved a lot of our problems.

I giggled. "I chose the wrong horse for that," I said out loud to Sandy.

"Abby," Mr. Hennessy's voice was sharp. "I think you're out of your mind."

"I wouldn't be surprised," I said, just as sharply. "This has been a terrible time."

18

Mr. Hennessy called hounds with a single short note of his horn. "This lot split again from the main pack earlier this afternoon," he said in a lower voice. "I think they're hoping to find that smart old dog fox that gave us such a great run earlier this year. You remember. Everyone else has gone on home."

He gestured for me to follow and started jogging his horse across the field. Sandy moved carefully away from the hounds and jogged comfortably along behind.

"I heard about Russ getting hurt this morning," Mr. Hennessy said, half over his shoulder. "Have you had any word about him?"

"Meg called. Just a little while ago. He's going to be okay."

Bill Hennessy nodded. The horses' hoofs whispered on the soft surface as we turned onto an unpaved road. There were pumpkins that seemed to glow with an orange light of their own as we jogged past the browns and golds of the cornfields beside us.

"I've known a few horses like that," Mr. Hennessy said, nodding his head toward Sandy. "I was talking to Russ about him just last night."

I had nothing to say. I had run out of all the words I knew.

"I've known more than a few horses that wouldn't jump a course of show fences if their lives depended on it. They do it a while, and then one day they've had enough. They get bored doing the same thing over and over." Another quick note on the horn brought a wandering hound romping back to join the others.

More silence from me. I kept my eyes on the happy hounds, their laughing expressions, and long, swinging ears. It was nice to see joy again. It had been a while.

"On the other hand," he went on slowly, "there are some of those that make useful hunting horses."

I nodded. Just once. Waiting and hoping for him to tell me the answer I'd come to believe might give Sandy a last chance.

"Good horses," Bill Hennessy repeated. "Brilliant horses, but real fighters if they don't like what they're doing." I began to whistle. Just a little bit. Under my breath. Kind of a whispery whistle.

"They're not the glory horses and that's for sure." Mr. Hennessy looked at Sandy. "They don't care about ribbons or fancy silver cups or trophies in the winner's circle. They don't even care if their owners don't get their names in the papers."

Our horses jogged along, Sandy now shoulder to shoulder with the bay, with hounds rippling around us.

"I suppose Russ and Meg wouldn't be asking a whole lot of money for such a horse," Mr. Hennessy said after a short silence. "Not now, under the circumstances. In fact, they could hardly give him away. Because I should

imagine we're talking about this Sandy horse you're riding. And I think I can guess why you're here."

"They're going to shoot him," I said.

"It might seem the sensible thing to do," he said.

Silence again, except for the hushed sound of the horses' hoofs and the pattering paws of the hounds.

"Still," Bill Hennessy said after a pause, "it could be a terrible waste of a good hunting horse. They're not that easy to find."

He shook his head wonderingly. "Here you are, riding cross-country and the horse going like a feather in the wind for you. And somehow you knew he'd be all right. At the same time, though, it would be worth your life, or anyone else's, to try to ride him through a show ring gate."

I nodded with a shudder of agreement.

Mr. Hennessy called to a lagging hound and shifted comfortably in his saddle. "I've ridden a lot of good horses through a lot of years, but I never rode a horse to a fence that gave me more confidence than Sandy did the day my horse fell and I had to stop hounds. I'll watch out for him. I don't want to end up in a hospital like Russ, but in his own way, Sandy's a great horse. I'd be glad to give him another chance. And if the horse works out in the hunting field the way I think he will, I'm going to have done myself a big favor."

Mr. Hennessy laughed and the great, booming sound was wonderful to hear. "I wouldn't want to push papers around an office desk all day, either. Same kind of thing, really."

The unpaved road curved and the small red hound van came into view, parked next to the hunt horse van.

Two kennel helpers in white coats were waiting beside the van, and as we rode closer, I saw one of them was Tommy.

"What in the world are you doing here?" I said to him dizzily.

"I guess I could ask you the same thing," he said, with his familiar grin. "Abby, I suppose you were always a little nuts. Maybe we both are."

He swung around to get the last hound safely into the van.

"Good kennel help is almost as hard to find as a good horse," Mr. Hennessy said. He smiled as he dismounted and started to unsaddle his horse. "Still. You never know. Some of you kids know how to use your heads. And get pretty good at what you do."

We had ridden in a wide circle. I could see the roof of High Hickory past the curve of one of the pasture walls where it dipped across the hill.

"You'll call Meg?" I asked desperately as Bill Hennessy started to load his horse into the van.

"I will," he said. "Tonight. I'll probably have a chance to talk to Russ, too. I'm going to stop by the hospital. And I'll tell him to stay off these rotten kids' horses." He smiled.

The bay's big hoofs thundered up the van ramp.

The wind was rising. Purple clouds were banking behind the trees, still shining in scarlet and copper colors in the slanting sun of late afternoon. A whirl of shimmering yellow leaves spun around us like a shower of gold coins. The wind brought the scent of apples and wood smoke.

I sat on Sandy in the dying sunlight with my hand on

his shoulder. I felt him stiffen as I started to turn him, and I nervously grabbed at his mane. But he did no more than whinny, just once, before swinging away at a touch of my heel.

I waved to Tommy and Mr. Hennessy and pressed Sandy into a canter. He moved almost soundlessly along the path in the woods that led back to High Hickory. I heard a faint rustling sound from the notepaper in the pocket of my jeans—the Dixons' telephone number.

I'd call them. Tonight. And tell them I'd ride Pumpkin for them in the coming show.

I let one hand rest on the back of Sandy's warm neck. He lengthened his sweeping stride. It was getting late, and both of us had a long way to go.

J
DOT

Doty, Jean
Slaughter

Dark horse

$10.

AUG 25
JUN 3
JUL 1 2
DEC
APR 2
MAY
JUN 1